One Brother in Danger . . .

I pulled out my cell and hit Joe's speed-dial number. He'd been AWOL all morning.

"Hello?" a voice answered. A gruff, deep voice.

Not Joe's voice.

I hung up immediately, my heart pounding in my chest. Why was some other dude answering my brother's phone? Where was Joe?

My cell phone rang. I checked the number—Joe's phone.

"I'm not that stupid," I muttered, hitting end. Obviously whoever had Joe's phone wanted to know who was calling him. . . . What was going on?

Where was my brother?

What had happened to Joe?

THE HARDY BOYS

UNDERCOVER BROTHERS®

Available from Simon & Schuster

THE HARDY BOYS

UNDERCOVER BROTHERS®

Super Mystery

#2 Kidnapped at the Casino

FRANKLIN W. DIXON

Aladdin Paperbacks
New York   London   Toronto   Sydney

❧ ALADDIN PAPERBACKS
An imprint of Simon & Schuster
Children's Publishing Division
1230 Avenue of the Americas
New York, NY 10020
Copyright © 2007 by Simon & Schuster, Inc.
All rights reserved, including the right of
reproduction in whole or in part in any form.
THE HARDY BOYS MYSTERY STORIES and HARDY BOYS UNDER-COVER BROTHERS are registered trademarks of Simon & Schuster, Inc.
ALADDIN PAPERBACKS and related logo are registered trademarks of Simon & Schuster, Inc.
Designed by Lisa Vega
The text of this book was set in Aldine 401BT.
Manufactured in the United States of America
First Aladdin Paperbacks edition May 2007
10 9 8 7 6 5 4 3 2 1
Library of Congress Control Number 2007922260
ISBN-13: 978-1-4169-3923-8
ISBN-10: 1-4169-3923-7

TABLE OF CONTENTS

1.

Smackdown at Sea

"Ouch," I said when I came to. I thought about it for a moment. "Ouch," I said again.

How was it possible to be so uncomfortable? I tried to stretch—and I couldn't. I couldn't move at all, in fact. I was trussed up like a calf at a rodeo. My hands and feet were tied together and then to each other, forcing me to stay hunched over in a fetal position, lying on my side.

No wonder I was uncomfortable.

Okay, think, I told myself. *How did I get here?* From the pain in my head, I guessed that someone had jumped me. I couldn't quite remember. Thinking made my head hurt more, so I decided to concentrate on just looking around.

It was dark. Pitch dark.

1

And there seemed to be a wall less than an inch in front of my face. And one next to my hands. And next to my legs.

I'm in a box, I realized. *Or maybe a trunk.* Not a large trunk, given how bent over I was. Definitely very mid-sized. I'm not claustrophobic, but this bothered me.

"Tied up," I muttered. "In a trunk. With a headache. And no idea how I got here." That pretty much summed it up. "Could be worse."

The big question was, where was Frank?

If I was trapped in a box, my brother couldn't be far away. Because the only reason something like this would happen to me was if an ATAC mission had gone bad. And I don't do ATAC missions alone. Whatever the mission is, Frank and I are in it together.

We had been recruited together by American Teens Against Crime. And we worked together for them. No matter what, I knew Frank had my back.

Unless I was supposed to have his back. If only I could remember.

"Frank?" I grunted as loudly as I could. News flash to me: When you're bent over with your face mashed against a wall, you can't make a very loud sound. Not a chance anyone was going to hear that.

2

Once I gave it more thought, I realized I probably shouldn't try yet, anyway. Whoever tied me up could still be out there and not know I was awake yet. Talking would just tip them off. And I'd lose whatever strategic advantage I had.

That's Frank's term. I don't think he uses it right. He likes to plan ahead, so he thinks "strategic advantage" means having something that might help him, something other people don't have. Like his stupid boots. His ugly black combat boots that he has to lace up around his ankles. I hate those boots. We had a bet about who could get up the cruise ship's climbing wall the fastest. Frank swore the boots were going to help him win. He was totally wrong about that.

Wait, I thought. *The cruise ship!*

Frank and I aren't usually on cruise ships.

And that's what finally made it all snap back into place. Frank and I were onboard the *Queen o' the Marina* cruise ship on a mission for ATAC. We were posing as deck waiters while we investigated a string of thefts on this ship over the past several months. Along with the typical jewelry, cash, and other valuables, the thieves had gotten their hands on some sensitive documents. A few of these had shown up on the black market, so ATAC wanted to know more about who had taken them. They figured that a couple of teenage waiters would be inconspicuous enough to fly under the radar and catch the crooks.

Apparently they were right. Frank and I figured out who the thieves were and got close to them . . . too close.

Suddenly I heard a tapping sound. It was faint, but I could just make it out. I concentrated, every muscle in my body tense. That tapping didn't sound random. I felt a grin break across my face. It was Morse code—taps with short and long pauses strung together. That had to be Frank. No one else I knew would use something that old. About a year ago, he made me learn how to decipher Morse code before we went on an ATAC assignment.

And now it was a strategic advantage.

"Hey Joe. R U there. Getting out soon. Thanks to boots." Boots? I was pretty sure that I had gotten the taps right. Maybe "boots" meant he had his feet free?

I wriggled around and got my finger to the side of the trunk. I tapped out, "Here. Tied up. Boots?" At least I think that's what I said.

"Boots kick butt" was all I got in response. Maybe Frank got hit over the head harder than I did. Dylan and Rosie were big dudes. They could hit pretty hard.

Dylan Krause and Roosevelt "Rosie" Lincoln. The names flooded back into my head. Those were the guys we needed to catch. They were the thieves. Dylan was one of the ship's engineers. Tall and lean, he looked more like one of the bridge crew, until you looked in his eyes. He knew gears, switches, and fuses, but not too much else. He was the kind of guy who would be fine if he didn't fall in with the wrong crowd.

Rosie was the wrong crowd. He was huge. The other waiters said he had been a college football star but had gotten into too much trouble for the pro football scouts to want him. Rosie had an ax to grind with everyone. Onboard, he was just a hired hand—security for casino night, broad back for lugging trunks around. Nobody suspected him of the burglaries. No one usually thinks of the big guy as the mastermind, but Rosie was it.

Pretty soon after we got onboard, Frank and I knew it was Dylan and Rosie. It took us two stops at idyllic little coastal towns and many sleepless nights of snooping to prove it. But we did. We had a folder full of evidence on them. We couldn't pass it off to ATAC until we got close to shore, but we were only a day away from the next stop, St. Yves.

One day too long. The details were still fuzzy in my scrambled egg of a brain, but Rosie and Dylan were waiting for Frank and me when we got off work that night. Right before I went down, I remember seeing . . .

The folder! They got the folder of evidence. I frantically tapped out a message to Frank: "The folder. Who has it." I waited for a response. And waited some more.

Tied up and in the dark, I didn't have much of a sense of time. Was it five minutes since I'd heard from Frank? Fifteen? Was he still out there at all?

Wham. Wham. Wham. Crack.

That didn't sound like Morse code. Had somebody heard us messaging each other? I waited, worrying.

"Joe." Frank's voice sounded close by. "Get as far back from the banging as you can."

"Banging?" I asked.

Wham! The whole side of the trunk rocked with the impact. "Oh," I said. I inched as far from that side as I could, which was all of about three inches. I hoped it was enough.

A little bit of light appeared as Frank plunged the saw tool on his Swiss Army knife through the side of the trunk. He did this four or five times, weakening the area around the lock. Then, with light streaming in, he hit the lock one final time and it fell off.

6

The trunk lid opened.

"You okay?" Frank asked as he cut the ropes around my wrists and ankles.

I stood up, stretching my back. "Peachy. Were you in a trunk too?" There was a lot of splintered wood lying around. "How did you get out?"

"It's all about the boots!" he bragged. I was so happy to see him and be un-pretzeled that I didn't even mind his gloating tone. "When they tied my legs together, they did it over my boots. So my feet could still move inside the boots. All I had to do was keep wriggling my feet out of them and I could kick the side out of my trunk."

I looked down at Frank's feet. There they were. The ugly black boots. Laced loosely up his ankles like always.

"You put your boots back on before you got me out of the trunk!" I cried, hitting him in the shoulder. "First save your brother, then put your boots back on."

"You weren't going anywhere." Frank looked me up and down. "Where's the folder?"

"I don't have it," I said. "Dylan and Rosie have it."

"We must be coming up on St. Yves," Frank said. "I guess we've been in the trunks all night. I think we're in the luggage holder—look at all the suitcases."

"They didn't want to hurt us, but they needed us out of the way long enough that they could get away with the folder," I guessed.

"What are we waiting for, then?" Frank asked. "We have to find them before they get off."

"Let's do it." I tore out of the luggage holder, with Frank right behind me.

"The Exercise Deck," I yelled over my shoulder to Frank. We ran through the long corridors of the passenger cabins, up some stairs, and through another set of corridors to get to the decks. We were pretty far down into the belly of the ship.

Before this assignment, I never knew the amount of fun they crammed onto the decks of big cruise ships. Above the passenger levels, there was a ton of decks—the Sun Deck, the Fun Deck, the Lido Deck, and so on. They ranged from serene oases where passengers relaxed with a drink and a book, to action-adventure settings with rock-climbing walls and water-park slides. Frank and I worked on the quiet decks and played on the exciting decks.

Right now, though, we were heading to the Exercise Deck, which included a jogging track that ringed most of the other decks. I figured we stood the best chance of seeing Dylan and Rosie from up there.

"Over there," Frank yelled to me, pointing up toward the start of the jogging track. "If we don't see them right away, we'll have a really good view of them getting off on the dock at St. Yves."

We dodged around the champagne pool, which had warm water with little light bubbles floating up from the bottom. I took the stairs two at a time up to the Exercise Deck. I didn't see Rosie and Dylan anywhere. I heard my brother pulling in air. After being stuck in a box for hours, we were both a little winded from the sprint. There were people all around, the same passengers we had been waiting on all week. But not the two people we were looking for.

"Frank!" One of the dancers from the onboard Broadway revue waved up at us from the Sun Deck below. Shanie. She was hot. And right now she was wearing a bikini and had her hair up in ponytails. Superhot. "What are you doing?" she called.

Frank looked flustered. Busting out of boxes, fighting bad guys—these things he could do. But talking to girls was beyond him. He's such a dork.

"Hey, Shanie!" I jumped in.

"Oh. Hi, Joe." She hadn't even noticed me.

"Any idea where Dylan and that big guy Rosie are? Have you seen them?" I asked.

"I think I saw them over by the reading lounges."

Frank and I turned to each other in concern. "The reading lounges. . . ," I started.

"That's over by the lifeboats," Frank finished. "They're not even going to wait for St. Yves. We've got to run." He took off toward the stairs.

"No, not that way!" I yelled after him. "We need to go to the wall. It's faster."

The climbing wall ran four stories up from the first open-air deck—which was also the deck with the boats. I ran to the top of the wall just as a pair of passengers successfully stepped off. The teen worker holding the safety ropes tried to stop me.

"Dude. You have to start down there." He pointed to the bottom of the wall, where a couple who wasn't going to make it to the top was about to bail on the whole thing. Frank and I would be safe going down once they were out of the way.

Frank jogged up behind me. "Good call. It's the fastest way."

"Seriously, dude. You can't just go down there," the worker said.

"We have to," Frank told him. "Don't worry— we work here." He stepped out onto the climbing wall and started down.

"We've got an urgent drink order that has to get in, so we're going down the fastest way possible," I added.

"Oh. Well, if you work here, why don't I just rappel you down?" the dude suggestion.

"Cool. Thanks." He handed me the ropes and helped me get strapped in. Frank had already disappeared down below our feet.

I looked over the edge of the platform. Frank was moving well until his foot slipped out. I told him those boots wouldn't work for climbing. The front was too square to use for toeholds. Frank was hanging by one hand!

"Frank. Hold on!" I yelled.

My brother looked up at me, sweating from the effort of hanging on with just one hand. He swung his boots around, trying to gain purchase. It didn't look good. He was facing a three-deck fall!

"Don't drop me," I told the worker. I stepped off the platform—and dropped like a stone. My heart skipped a beat. If I fell, I would probably take Frank with me.

The ropes pulled taut, and I stopped falling. "Sorry," the guy called down. "I'm used to pulling people up and there's no extra rope when you do that. . . ."

"It's fine. Let's go," I called back. The guy began lowering me again, slowly this time. As I got closer to Frank, his feet slipped out again. His body dropped, and his hand only just barely held on to the handhold.

I kicked off the wall, making myself swing out on

the rope. This way I could get behind my brother. I threw my arms under his, hugging him from behind. "Gotcha," I said.

Frank breathed a sigh of relief. "Thanks," he said. "I guess the boots are one out of two for life-saving feats."

"We're good to go," I called up to the dude at the top.

He lowered us the rest of the way to the bottom, and we took off toward the reading lounges—and the lifeboats.

It was easy to spot Rosie. He was just about to lower a lifeboat into the water. Frank didn't even slow down. He just launched himself at Rosie . . . and bounced off, landing on Dylan. Dylan took a swing, and Frank ducked.

I turned my attention to Rosie. The big guy leaned down to grab a lockbox near his feet. I figured it held today's haul and the folder we'd accumulated on them. He would want to dispose of that properly to make sure it didn't fall into the wrong hands.

"Not so fast, Rosie!" I ran toward him and jumped up, landing a nice straight kick in his chest. He fell back a little, but not enough. His giant mitt of a hand grabbed the back of my neck while his other moved under my arm. He was going to throw me off the boat!

"Stay out of my business, spy boy," he growled.

I twisted around, but I couldn't get any purchase. Luckily, Frank saw what was happening. With Dylan's hand wrapped around his ankle, trying to pull him away, Frank grabbed one of the lifeboat oars and smacked Rosie in the side of his knee.

Rosie bellowed in pain and let go of me. I fell, slamming hard on the deck. Rosie grabbed the front of the oar to pull it from Frank's hands. Meanwhile, Dylan ran to the lockbox, picking it up.

I flipped myself to my feet and used a low round-house kick to sweep Rosie's feet out from under him. Big guys fall hard. Or at least that's what it looked like when he landed on Dylan. Dylan squawked and let the lockbox go. It slid across the highly polished wooden deck, right to a security officer who had come over to stop the fight.

Frank and I stood up as the officer pulled his gun on the four of us. I wasn't worried. Once they opened that box up, they would know it was Rosie and Dylan they wanted, not my brother and me.

I grinned at Frank. "Nothing like a relaxing cruise vacation," I said.

2.

College Life

"Frank, honey, will you get the paper?" Mom asked the next morning. She was sitting at the kitchen table with a huge mug of coffee, looking just as tired as she did every other day of the week. She's not a morning person.

"Of course," I said, giving her a smile. Every morning, she asked me to get the paper, and every morning, I did. It was like a little ritual or something.

I pushed open the door and stepped out into the crisp early autumn air. The sun was shining, the leaves on the maple tree had just started to turn red, and the sky was impossibly clear and blue. I grabbed the newspaper from the grass, and stopped.

Something was wrong.

The plastic bag wrapped around the newspaper was intact, but it was blue. It's usually clear. And the paper was folded into more of a square shape than usual. I kept my back to the door and took a look. I couldn't put my finger on it, but something was bothering me. So I grabbed the end of the plastic and pulled it open.

A folder fell out from inside the newspaper. It was black, with a big neon green question mark in the middle.

I opened it up, looking for a disk. And there it was. I grinned.

"What's that?" asked a voice in my ear.

I jumped, and turned to see Aunt Trudy standing about two feet away. I couldn't believe I hadn't heard her come outside. I guess she's pretty stealthy for an old-ish lady.

"Oh, it's a—"

Aunt Trudy didn't let me finish. She just snatched the disk from my hand. My stomach gave a nervous lurch—I knew what the disk was. It was a mission assignment from ATAC. They had hidden it in the paper because they knew I was the one who picked it up every morning. But now Aunt Trudy had it in her hands, and if Aunt Trudy discovered that Joe and I were ATAC agents, well, we wouldn't be ATAC agents for long.

"Kidnapped?" Aunt Trudy said, squinting at the disk.

I glanced at the thin cardboard cover wrapped around the mission disk. It matched the folder, with the big question mark in the middle. But the disk had the title KIDNAPPED floating over the question mark.

I grinned. ATAC always manages to hide its identity.

"Cool—I've been wanting to try that game." I reached for the disk.

Aunt Trudy frowned. "Somebody put a game in the newspaper? For free?" she asked suspiciously.

"It's probably a trial. You know, for one-use only," I explained. And I wasn't even lying. ATAC's mission disks did destroy themselves after one use. That way, no one could track them.

"What's in the folder?" she asked.

I shrugged. "All the promotional stuff to get you to buy the game."

Reluctantly, Aunt Trudy handed over the disk. I brought the paper inside to Mom, then headed straight upstairs to Joe's room.

My slacker brother was still asleep. I jerked the pillow out from under his head on my way to the computer.

"Hey," Joe protested as his head smacked onto the mattress.

I yanked the blinds open, spilling bright sunlight into the room.

"You suck," Joe muttered.

"I know, but this is worth getting up for," I told him. "We've got a new assignment."

Joe was out of bed in less than a second, all the sleep gone from his eyes. "Gimme," he said. He grabbed the disk and stuck it into his computer. He's always just as psyched as I am to find out what awesome adventure ATAC is sending us on next. The computer screen went black for a few seconds, and then a photograph appeared. A girl's face—a *pretty* girl's face. I could feel myself clamming up already. Did we have to go talk to this girl for the mission? Because I can't do that, not without looking like a complete idiot.

"Kathy Boutry," said a deep voice. "Age nineteen. A sophomore at Hewlett University, a member of the soccer team, president of the Journalism Club—"

"Total hottie," Joe put in with a grin.

"No known enemies," the voice was saying. "So why did she vanish without a trace?"

I frowned. "She's gone?"

"Kathy left for class yesterday morning and hasn't

17

been seen since," the voice went on. "Campus security had no reports of anything unusual occurring at the time, and a thorough search of the college grounds has turned up nothing."

"Still," Joe said, "it doesn't really sound like an ATAC case. Maybe she just took off."

"Or maybe somebody grabbed her. Just because no one saw anything weird doesn't mean—"

"Shh!" Joe shushed me. "It's just getting good."

A newspaper article had appeared on-screen. Followed by another, and another, and another. All different papers. But all had the same byline: Kathy Boutry. "Kathy isn't a minor, and she hasn't been missing for forty-eight hours, so she cannot be reported to police as a missing person," the voice said. "However, the reason this case has come to our attention is simple: Kathy is a reporter who frequently investigates criminal activity. ATAC believes she was abducted in order to prevent her from exposing illegal behavior."

"If that's true, she could be in real danger," I said. "Criminals tend to kill whistle-blowers."

"Kathy's notepad was recovered from her desk at the *Hewlett Horn*—the university newspaper," the voice went on. "It appears that she was working on several different stories. It's up to you to figure out which—if any—could have led to her abduction. We feel that the two of you will have an easier time fitting in at Kathy's college than an adult investigator would."

"Piece of cake," Joe said. He leaned back in his chair and stretched his arms over his head, yawning.

"In the attached folder you will find a map of the campus and Kathy's class schedule," the voice said.

I flipped open the question mark folder and found the map, the schedule, Kathy's notepad, and a small stack of money for us to use while on the case.

"Statistics show that most kidnapping victims are killed within three days of their abduction," the voice went on. "If the criminal element learns that law enforcement is closing in, they are likely to kill their hostage rather than let her be rescued. Kathy Boutry's life is in your hands. As always, this mission is top secret. This disk will be reformatted in five seconds."

A digital clock appeared on-screen. It counted down from 5 to 1, and then The Killers came blaring from the computer speakers.

Joe reached over and turned down the volume.

"We better hope it's a piece of cake," I told him. "Kathy's life depends on it."

FROM KATHY'S NOTEPAD:

Tony Calenda—election scam

Stuffing boxes?

*Background: Calenda serves as sophomore election
 commissioner. Frat brother of presidential
 candidate. Writes disparaging editorial of opposition
 candidate. Overheard in dining hall: " I control
 election. "

*Need: source to confirm ballot box stuffing

*Check: campus rules governing student elections.
 Who oversees student gov't.?
 Are the ballots still around?

MetaChem dumping

Toxic waste?

*Background: MetaChem manufactures polyurethane.
 Benzene found in trace amounts in Hammonton Lake.
 Benzene used to make adipic acid for polyurethane
 manufacturing. Possible dumping of by-products
 upstream?

*Check: other possible sources of contamination—
 leaks from other areas?

*Saul Gold, CEO

*Does this contaminate drinking water? Pulitzer!

<u>Slots rigged?</u>

Check complaints from old-timers.

"College girls!" Joe said happily as he hopped off his motorcycle in front of Kathy's dorm at Hewlett University. We had driven down here on our bikes as soon as Mom had left for work. We didn't tell her we were skipping school that day, and we certainly didn't tell Aunt Trudy. But ATAC would call and let the principal know we were on a mission. They had an arrangement with the Bayport High School administration. We could skip classes whenever ATAC missions required us to, as long as we always made up all the work.

"Focus, Joe," I told my brother. "We don't have time for flirting."

"Who's flirting?" Joe asked. "I can just look. That doesn't take any time."

I shook my head and pulled the map of the campus from my backpack. While Joe studied the females, I studied the layout of the place. "The dorms are that way," I said, pointing to the west. "Kathy's room is in Kellerman Hall."

I led the way down the brick pathway.

"So we're checking her room why?" Joe asked, following me.

"To see what her roommate knows about this

Tony Calenda guy," I said. "Kathy's notes talk about a student election, so the dude probably goes here."

"Kathy has notes on two other stories too," Joe pointed out.

"Yeah, but she goes to college here, she lives on campus, and she was last seen leaving for class," I said. "This is the obvious place to start."

We'd reached Kellerman. It was three stories high, and Kathy's room was on the top floor. "Here we are," Joe said, knocking on the door of room 326.

A short, African-American girl opened the door. "Yeah?" she asked.

"Hi . . ." My voice trailed off.

"We're friends of Kathy's," Joe jumped in. He's used to me being tongue-tied around girls. "You're her roommate, right? She told me your name, but I forgot it. Sorry."

"Beth." She raised an eyebrow. "And you look a little young to be hanging out with Kathy. How do you know her?"

"My brother went to high school with her. Right, Frank?" Joe asked.

Nice. Throw it all on me, I thought, glaring at him. "Um . . . yeah," I said.

I guess Beth decided that I looked old enough, because she opened the door and waved us inside.

One side of the room was filled with pillows and stuffed animals. On the other side, newspaper and magazine articles were taped all over the wall. It was pretty obvious which side belonged to Kathy Boutry.

"Kathy's not here," Beth said. "And don't ask me where she is, 'cause I don't know."

"She's missing?" Joe asked. "Since when?"

"Yesterday," Beth replied. "I told the campus security guys, but honestly I'm not that worried. You know Kathy."

I wasn't sure what to say. I *didn't* know Kathy. But luckily, Beth didn't expect an answer.

"I bet she's just off on one of her investigations," Beth went on. She plopped down on her bed and grabbed a little stuffed dog. She tossed it back and forth in her hands as she talked. "She couldn't care less about school. I don't think it would even occur to her that she's missing classes or anything."

"Do you think the editor of the newspaper would know where she is?" I asked.

Beth snorted. "Which one?"

I shot a look at Joe. He shrugged. "Um, the school paper?" I said. "That's who she's writing for now, right?"

"No. I mean, yes, sometimes." Beth got bored with the dog and put it down. "But she says that's just amateur garbage. She only cares about the real papers. She's always sending story ideas off to the county paper. And last week she started saying she had a story for the *Press of Atlantic City*. Seriously, I think if she could get a gig working there, she would quit school."

"Still, wouldn't she call you if she was going to be out all night?" Joe asked.

"Doubtful." Beth shrugged. "She stopped telling me about her so-called investigative journalism after I told her student adviser about the trespassing thing."

"What trespassing thing?" I asked.

"You know, that chemical place. She thought they were doing something wrong, so she started hanging around there. The security guys kept kicking her off the grounds for trespassing." Beth grinned. "So then she went and got a temp job there answering phones. But the security guy recognized her and had her escorted out like a criminal. Isn't that awesome? She was, like, stalking the chemical company. Isn't that just like her?"

I laughed, as if I knew what she was talking about.

"Kathy mentioned she was doing a story about an election," Joe said. "A student election?"

"Yeah. So?" Beth asked.

"So, uh, do you know anything about that?" I asked.

"Was there some scandal?" Joe put in. "Kathy said the ballot boxes were stuffed or something. By Tony Calendar."

"Calenda," Beth corrected him. "There were some rumors. And Kathy followed him around for a while to try to find proof. But she hasn't mentioned it lately. Why?"

"Do you know what dorm Tony lives in?" I asked.

"He's not in the dorms—he lives at his frat." Beth was frowning. "What's your deal, anyway? Why do you care about Tony?"

"I don't," I said quickly.

"We're just looking for Kathy," Joe added.

"Well, she's not here. And she is definitely not at Tony's." Beth stood up. "I have a class in ten minutes."

I could take a hint. We said our good-byes and left. Downstairs in the dorm lobby, Joe turned to me. "Now what?"

"I guess we find Tony's fraternity," I said slowly. "There was a frat row on the map, right next to that little nature preserve. Maybe we can just knock on the doors and ask if he's there."

"Let's do it," my brother said, jogging off toward the bikes.

Joe wasn't jogging anymore by the time we reached the fourth house on frat row. He was just dragging himself along behind me, complaining about how hungry he was. He's always hungry— Aunt Trudy calls him the human vacuum. "This is taking forever," Joe mumbled as I checked off the Phi Gamma house on the campus map. Tony wasn't a brother there, and nobody seemed sure which frat he belonged to. For a guy at the center of a college scandal, he didn't seem very well known. "I'll do the talking at this one," Joe announced, heading up the brick walkway to the Delta Psi house.

"Joe," I called after him. "Wait!"

He ignored me, as usual. He just grabbed the big brass knocker on the door and banged it loudly.

I followed him to the door. "Uh, Joe?"

"What?" he yelled over the sound of his own knocking.

"This is a sorority house," I said. "Look." I pointed to banner hanging from one upstairs window. It read: SISTERS UNITE.

"Oh." Joe stopped banging on the door. But it was too late. An Asian girl with an annoyed expression on her face had already yanked open the door.

"What?" she asked.

"Um . . . sorry about the noise," Joe said. He put

his typical flirtatious smile on his face. "We're trying to find a girl who's missing, and it seemed like this was a good place to ask for assistance."

She frowned at him, and then she turned to me. "Who is this missing girl?"

"Her name is Kathy Boutry," I told her. "We have reason to believe that a guy named Tony Calenda may be involved."

The girl ran her eyes from my head down to my toes. "Are you a cop?" she asked.

"No, he's just a dork," Joe said helpfully. "Do you know Tony?"

"Yeah, I've seen him around," she replied. "I doubt he would be involved in something like kidnapping or . . . whatever."

"Do you know which frat he belongs to?" I asked.

"Omega Rho," she said. "It's the last house on the block."

"Great. Thanks." Joe gave her another smile. "Hey, you don't have anything to eat in there, do you?"

"Excuse me?" she said.

"I'm starving," Joe said.

She just rolled her eyes and closed the door on us.

"That was rude," Joe muttered as I led the way back to the sidewalk.

"We should take the bikes," I said. "It looks like a long walk."

A few minutes later we parked at the curb in front of the Omega Rho house. It was the biggest one, and it was the last one on the incredibly long block of fraternity and sorority houses. Behind it ran the nature preserve, which just looked like a regular forest to me.

"Who knew there would be so many frats?" I said. "I'm surprised anybody is left to live in the dorms."

"Look, we know he belongs to this one," Joe said. "We know he's a brother here. Let's just go get dinner."

"Kathy's time is running out," I reminded him.

Joe sighed and got off his motorcycle. "I know. It's just hard to believe she would be in danger from some stupid frat guy who wants to hide a student government thing."

"If he took Kathy, that makes him more than some stupid frat guy," I said. "It makes him a kidnapper. It makes him dangerous."

"You're right." Joe went up to the door and pounded on it. The thick wooden door opened, and a huge guy with a buzz cut scowled at us.

"Hey," I greeted him. "Is Tony here?"

He grunted and walked away, leaving the door open.

"Let me handle this. I speak Neanderthal," Joe

cracked. "I believe he just said, 'Come on in.' " He stepped inside, and I followed. The place was swanky, with a pool table, two huge vintage video games, and a supersweet entertainment system in the living room. But I knew Mom would say it needed a woman's touch. I think that's code for "It needs to be cleaned." There were jackets, shoes, and books flung all over the place, along with a few dirty towels and some half-eaten sandwiches. You could tell a bunch of guys lived there.

The question was, where was Tony?

"First place you look for a dude is in the kitchen," Joe said. He made his way through the living room, stepped over a life-size dummy in a football jersey, and went into the dining room on the other side.

I stopped to look at the dummy. It was one of those CPR training dummies, but somebody had painted blood all over it and slashed its jersey. "I hope he's from the opposing team," I muttered. Still, it was pretty violent.

I glanced around the room. Two huge guys were playing some kind of game on the big flat screen. They were shooting at each other on-screen and shouting at each other in reality. One blew the other's head off in the game, hooting in victory.

These guys definitely like their violent video games, I

thought. *And the one who answered the door didn't seem to have any great people skills. And we're walking right into the middle of their house to find out if one of their brothers is a criminal.*

Suddenly this didn't seem like such a terrific idea. I jogged after my brother.

"Joe," I hissed, grabbing his sleeve, "how do we know they're not all in on it?"

He looked at me, then raised his eyes to Big and Bigger, who were just starting a new game in the living room. "You mean, they might all be willing to nab Kathy in order to cover their brother's butt?"

"Yeah."

Joe hesitated. "I guess we'll just have to try to get Tony alone," he said. "We won't mention Kathy's name."

"Okay." I figured we could come up with some cover story if we found the guy. "Is he in the kitchen?"

"I don't know. There's some kind of contest going on," Joe said.

I peered over his shoulder. Three guys were stuffing saltine crackers into their mouths while a fourth one timed them. Their cheeks were bulging, and their eyes were watering, but those dudes just kept shoving crackers in.

"Wow," Joe said beside me. "That's impressive. I think that blond guy is up to twelve crackers."

I just stared at him.

"What?" my brother said. "It's hard. You try eating that many saltines without a drink to wash them down. They turn to mortar in your mouth."

"How do we know if one of them is Tony?" I asked.

Joe shrugged and kept watching. I spotted a middle-aged woman heading out the kitchen door. "Be right back," I said to Joe. I edged around the saltine brothers and caught up with her. "Excuse me," I called. "I'm looking for Tony Calenda. Do you know if one of these guys is him?"

"Nope, he's not in there," she replied.

"What are they doing, anyway?" I asked.

She chuckled. "Honey, I'm paid to cook for them and wash the dishes. That's it. I don't even try to interpret the weird things they do." She left, and I turned back just in time to see the fourth guy call time. The eaters all collapsed onto the kitchen chairs and grabbed for their water glasses.

I went back over to Joe. The brothers were all so busy trying to dissolve the crackers in their mouths that they didn't even look at us.

"You know, I'm getting the feeling that these guys aren't in on the Kathy Boutry kidnapping," Joe commented. "They don't even seem to care that a couple of total strangers are wandering around their house.

Watch." He went over to the table and grabbed a half-empty sleeve of crackers. "You guys mind if I snag some? I'm starving," he said.

The brothers all grunted. The fourth one glanced at him, then at me, then went back to tallying up how many saltines each guy had eaten.

"See?" Joe said, stuffing a cracker in his mouth. "If they had something to hide, they'd be beating me up right now." He held out the cracker sleeve to me.

"Let's just keep looking," I told him.

We headed for the wide staircase and started up. Another frat brother was coming down, but he just glanced at us and kept going. At the top was a long hallway with a bunch of bedrooms. I stuck my head into the first open door and nodded at the guy sprawled on his bed watching TV.

"Dude, you know where Tony Calenda is?" I asked.

"Second to last door on the right," he said.

"Thanks." I walked down to the door and knocked. No answer.

"If he's not here, we can search his room," Joe said. He glanced around to make sure nobody was watching, then opened the door. We slipped inside quickly . . . and saw a big guy climbing out the window!

3.

Blackjack!

I started to yell, but Frank clapped his hand over my mouth. "Heeef gebbim mmwee," I protested.

"I know he's getting away," Frank replied. "But if you let him know that we saw him, he'll just run even faster. Right now he thinks he's sneaking out with nobody noticing." He moved over to the window and peered out after Tony. "He's cutting through the woods."

"He's probably got a car parked on the street behind it," I said.

My brother took off down the hall of the frat house, running for the stairs. "Where do you think he's going?" Frank asked as he burst out the front door onto the porch. "It has to be someplace he doesn't want his brothers to know about, right?

33

SUSPECT PROFILE

Name: Anthony "Tony" Calenda

Hometown: New York, NY

Physical Description: Age 20, 5'11", 180 lbs., dark brown hair, green eyes

Occupation: Student at Hewlett University

Background: Son of Michael Calenda, head of Futuro Management Consulting

Suspicious behavior: Listed in Kathy Boutry's notepad; boasted of controlling student elections; was discovered sneaking out of his own room through the window.

Suspected of: Fixing student government election; kidnapping Kathy Boutry.

Possible motive: To prevent Kathy from exposing his election tampering.

Why else would he climb out the window?"

I nodded, getting it. "So following him might help us more than questioning him," I said.

"Hopefully he'll lead us straight to the place he's holding Kathy." Frank hurried over to his bike, parked at the curb. I climbed on my own bike and powered up. We raced back down Fraternity Row and rounded the corner, following the tree line.

When we reached the other side of the small nature preserve, I spotted a black Mercedes convertible pulling out in front of us.

"It was nice of Tony to put the top down," I said into the mic in my helmet. "Now we've got a positive ID on him—that is definitely the guy we saw inside."

"Seems like this case will be a piece of cake after all," Frank's voice answered through the speaker near my ear.

I revved my motorcycle and sped up to keep Tony's car in my sight. I would be happy to get Kathy back to her dorm, and I'd be even happier to get Tony thrown in jail. What kind of loser kidnaps somebody just to keep his name out of the paper? And what kind of idiot thinks he'll get away with it? It was amazing this guy had gotten into college at all!

Tony's car took a sharp turn and raced up an entrance ramp onto the Atlantic City Expressway. I felt a jolt of surprise. Somehow I'd figured that he was keeping Kathy nearby. I leaned into the turn and followed him up onto the traffic-clogged highway. Tony's car was already several car lengths ahead—but that's no problem when you're on a motorcycle. I weaved through the traffic until there was only a VW Bug between me and him. Frank pulled up beside me.

"Where's he going?" my brother asked through the radio.

"No clue," I replied. "We'll just have to wait and see."

Wherever it was, it was taking a long time, I thought half an hour later. We were still on the Atlantic City Expressway, still stuck in Atlantic City traffic. Was Tony keeping Kathy in the city somewhere?

But he kept on going even after all the other cars had turned off the road. We had been following the Mercedes for forty minutes by the time Tony took an exit with a sign for OLDE TYME.

The exit led right to the circular driveway of a six-story-high hotel that was built to look like a big Mississippi River steamboat. Tony pulled his convertible up to the front doors and hopped out, snatching a valet ticket from a guy dressed like a sailor. He went inside.

Frank and I drove our bikes past the door and pulled over to the side of the driveway. "What is this place?" I asked my brother, pulling off my helmet.

He squinted up at the sign over the entrance. "'Olde Tyme Resort and Casino,'" he read. "Never heard of it."

"Atlantic City is only twenty miles away. Why would anybody go to a casino out here when they can go to all the different casinos there?" I asked.

Frank shrugged. "Maybe if they're tired of driving they can just stop here first. Or maybe they like gambling but don't like how crowded A.C. is. Or maybe they like—"

"Okay, okay, whatever," I said. "Why is Tony here?"

"I don't know," Frank admitted. "We'd better get inside and see what he's doing."

"Uh, Frank?" I said. "You have to be twenty-one to go into a casino. And ATAC didn't give us fake IDs along with Kathy's campus map."

"Well, ATAC didn't know we'd end up at a casino," Frank said.

"I guess they need to give us fake IDs to always keep with us in case of emergency," I cracked.

"Yeah. That'll happen," Frank said sarcastically. My brother nodded at a small wooden sign that read SELF-PARKING. A smaller driveway led down to an underground parking garage. "We'll have an easier time of it if we don't use the valets," Frank said. "I don't know who checks IDs, but we'll just have to avoid them."

We revved our bikes and headed down to the garage. "How did Tony get in?" I asked once we had parked. "Kathy's notes say he's a sophomore. He's not twenty-one either."

Frank shrugged. "He's not the most honest guy in the world. He probably has a fake ID."

"I bet they pay more attention to the elevators, so let's take the emergency stairs," I suggested."

On the main floor, the stairs opened right into the casino. The whole place was loud—slot machines ringing and beeping, brightly colored lights flashing, and some kind of ragtime music playing in the background. "Check it out—shops," Frank said, pointing down a hallway to our left. I spotted a bunch of fancy-looking stores with big picture windows, decorated as if they were the shops along an old-fashioned Main Street.

"O-kay." I shot my brother a questioning look.

"We need to buy sport coats," Frank said, leading the way toward the little mini-mall. "If we're wearing jackets, we'll look respectable, blend in more."

"You mean we'll look old."

Frank laughed. "I just mean Security won't notice us."

We passed three boutiques with women's clothes before we finally found a golf shop for men. They had about five sport coats on a rack in the back. We found the ones that fit us the best, and Frank slapped down some of the money from ATAC. I bet they never thought we'd go clothes shopping with it!

"I look good," I commented, checking out my ensemble in the store mirror. The jacket was dark blue, and it made my jeans seem a little classier. "Maybe I should get a hat or something too."

"Don't push it," Frank said, rolling his eyes.

I grinned and went back out into the hallway. We made our way to the main casino, carefully avoiding the security guards. One of the things I had learned working undercover for ATAC is that as long as you act confident, people don't usually question you.

"Let's hope Tony is in the casino," Frank said. "If he went up into the hotel, we'll never find him."

I glanced around, taking in the place. To my left were a bunch of gaming tables—blackjack, poker, roulette, all that stuff. To my right were rows and rows of slot machines with shiny metal arms that you pull down to spin the wheels. The slot machines were mostly taken by older people who sat around with big plastic buckets full of nickels and quarters, feeding them into the machines. A younger crowd was at the gambling tables.

"There he is," my brother said suddenly. "Black-jack."

I peered through the room and finally spotted Tony Calenda at a blackjack table with three other people. He sat scowling at his cards, a huge pile of chips in front of him. "He's *gambling*?" I said. "What about Kathy?"

"I don't know." Frank frowned. "Why did he have to climb out the window just to come to a casino? Who cares if he wants to play blackjack?"

"Maybe he's here to meet somebody," I suggested. "Maybe he's just waiting for his accomplice to show up."

"I guess we'd better keep him under surveillance," Frank muttered. "It won't be easy, though. I don't think we can gamble away ATAC's money."

"We can just watch," I said. "Lots of people are standing around watching."

Frank nodded. "I'll hang out at the roulette table behind Tony," he said. "You hang near Tony's table."

"Good idea. We'd be more conspicuous together," I agreed. Frank went over to fake-watch the roulette, and I joined a middle-aged couple who were watching Tony's game. Tony was playing the odds—holding on sixteen, hitting on fifteen. I figured he must've read *Blackjack for Idiots* or something. But it wasn't working. The dealer raked in Tony's chips after every hand.

A big, middle-aged guy in a Mickey Mouse shirt elbowed his way past me and sat down next to Tony. "Hey, yo, chips here," he said. He tossed four hundred-dollar bills onto the blackjack table, and the dealer gave him a pile of chips.

"Hey, buddy. How's the table?" Mickey asked Tony. Tony just winced. "That good, huh?" The guy laughed loudly.

But I could tell that Tony wasn't wincing at the table. This guy was already on Tony's last nerve.

The dealer tossed out the cards. Tony was showing a seven on top, but from the look on his face, he had something like an eight or a nine underneath. Low odds for winning.

But Mickey was having a little celebration in his seat. "All right. Blackjack," he bellowed. The dealer paid out and moved on to Tony.

Tony looked at his down card and waved off the dealer. The dealer flipped his own cards, showing a seventeen. Tony punched the table, hard. "This sucks," he snapped.

"Sir. . . ," the dealer began.

"What?" Tony flipped his card at the dealer, sneering. I could see that he'd had sixteen. Once again, he'd lost.

His pile of chips was down to only two. *Two hundred dollars is still more than I'd be willing to risk,* I thought.

The dealer cleared the table, and the players anted up. Mickey pounded Tony on the back.

"Don't worry about it, my friend, the worm's gotta turn sometime." Tony glared at him, but the dude didn't seem to notice.

I yawned and looked at my watch. I like black-jack, but it's not much fun watching other people play. And Tony wasn't very good at it. The Mickey Mouse guy wasn't bad, but that only seemed to make Tony madder.

"Double down," Tony told the dealer. He tossed his last chip in.

Good, maybe he'll lose, I thought. This was way too boring. When Tony was out of chips, maybe he would do something else, something more inter-esting. Like take us to Kathy Boutry.

I turned to look for Frank. He was standing next to a gorgeous girl in a short black dress. But he was oblivious. Typical. My brother is just not good with women. I must've gotten all the talent in that department.

"You took my ten, loser." Tony's voice pulled my attention back to the game. He was nose-to-nose with the Mickey Mouse guy, yelling at top volume.

"Calm down, kid, we're all playing the dealer here," Mickey Mouse told him.

"Calm down?" Tony repeated. His voice was pretty much the opposite of calm.

"Frank," I called to my brother. "Some help?"

Frank made his way toward me, pushing through the little knot of people watching the game.

"Looks like you're out of chips," Mickey Mouse said. "I guess you're done."

Tony pushed away from the blackjack table so hard that his stool toppled over backward. He didn't bother to pick it up, or to apologize.

"*You're* done," he growled. He grabbed the older guy's shoulder and cocked his fist.

Tony was about to flatten Mickey Mouse!

FRANK

4.
A Bad Bet

I had no time to think. I just tossed my Coke through the air, hoping it would land on Tony and not the other guy.

Perfect, I thought as the soda spattered Tony's shirt. He backed up, surprised, and forgot about hitting the Mickey Mouse man.

"I'm really sorry—" I started.

Tony ignored me. He just turned and stalked out of the casino. I shot a look at Joe, and he nodded. We followed Tony, catching up to him just before he reached the front doors.

"Excuse me," I said. "Do you know—"

"No," Tony barked, sneering at me. It was all we needed. While his attention was on me, Joe lifted Tony's wallet from the pocket of his khakis.

"Hey," he snapped, turning on my brother.

"Hey," Joe replied with a friendly smile. "I bet there's a fake ID in here, huh? Should I tell Gigantor over there, or would you rather come have a talk with my brother and me?"

Tony glanced at the huge security guard near the door, who was staring at us pretty hard. "I don't mind having a talk," he replied.

"Good. Let's go grab a drink," I said. I led the way to a restaurant across from the main casino. It had small, wrought-iron tables and was decorated to look like an old-fashioned ice-cream parlor.

"Give me my wallet," Tony demanded as we sat down.

"Not right now," I told him. "First we have a few questions for you."

"Who are you guys?" he asked. "Why should I tell you anything?"

"We're looking for Kathy Boutry, and we think you have her," I said, cutting straight to the point.

Tony's mouth dropped open. "Excuse me?"

"Kathy. Where is she?" I asked.

"How should I know?" Tony began to laugh. "Are you serious? My fraternity brothers didn't send you?"

Joe was frowning. "Why would they send us?"

"Oh, they're all sensitive about my so-called gambling problem," Tony said. He flagged down a waiter. "Get me a root beer. And whatever these dudes want."

I ordered iced tea, but Joe just waved the guy off. I could tell my brother wasn't happy. "You have a gambling problem?" he asked Tony.

"No." Tony squirmed in his seat, blushing a little. "Okay, maybe. I just like to gamble. What's the big deal?"

"It's illegal until you're twenty-one," I pointed out. "Also, you lost more than a thousand dollars tonight. Sounds like a problem to me."

"Whatever. I can afford it." Tony shrugged. "My father makes tons of money. He'll never notice a few thousand missing."

"Wow. Must be nice," Joe said sarcastically. "I guess your frat brothers don't agree. Is that why you had to sneak out of your room? And go to a casino in the middle of nowhere?"

"Yeah. So what?" Tony crossed his arms. "It's none of their business, anyway. And it's none of your business. Who are you guys?"

"We're Kathy's friends," I said. "You still haven't told us where she is."

"I told you, I don't know. That chick is nuts,"

Tony said. "She used to follow me around all the time, asking questions and stuff. I figured she was into me. So I brought her here, like, on a date. I even gave her money to play the slots. After that, she totally ignored me. I haven't seen her since."

"So you think she's nuts for dumping you?" Joe asked, sounding amused.

"She didn't dump me. It was only our first date. Before that, she was just stalking me or something."

"She was investigating you," I corrected him. "She's a reporter, and she knew you fixed the student government election."

Tony jumped up. "I did not," he snapped. "There's no proof of that."

"Especially not now, with Kathy missing," I said. "Did she find proof? Is that why you kidnapped her?"

"You're crazy." Tony looked seriously upset. "I didn't kidnap anyone. I didn't even know she was a reporter." He sat back down. "Just because I like to gamble doesn't mean I'm a kidnapper. I wouldn't do something like that. I barely knew the girl. Why don't you call the cops if she's missing?"

"You want us to call the police?" I repeated.

"Yeah, if you can't find your friend."

He was being totally honest. He wanted us to

alert the authorities. I shot Joe a look, and I could see that he was thinking the same thing I was: Guilty people don't suggest calling the cops. Guilty people try to avoid the police at all costs. Tony really didn't have Kathy.

We were back to square one—no Kathy. And no suspects.

"Now what?" I sighed, leaning back on the fake ice-cream parlor chair. Tony Calenda had just left, after getting his wallet back from Joe. "Tony was our top suspect."

"He was our only suspect," Joe pointed out. "Let me look at Kathy's notepad again."

I pulled the notepad out of my backpack, and Joe flipped through it. "We should head back to the college," I said. "People don't just disappear—someone must have seen her."

"What about these other stories she was working on?" Joe asked. "That MetaChem place? And check it out: 'slots rigged?' I bet she was talking about this place, the casino."

"Let me see," I said. I glanced at the page where Kathy had scrawled a note about complaints from old-timers. "Olde Tyme Casino, complaints from old-timers. I guess that could be what she meant," I said thoughtfully. "But it's not very clear."

"Sure it is," Joe argued. "Tony said she came here with him, and then she totally blew him off. It's because she found a better story than some college election scandal. She found a story here, at the casino. Look, it says the slots are rigged."

I frowned down at Kathy's scribbled note. It did mention rigged slots, but what did that even mean? She made no mention of a casino. "For all we know, she's still talking about the election here. Tony rigged the ballot boxes so the slots open in the student government went to his friends."

Joe rolled his eyes. "We're already here. We might as well check out the casino."

"I think we need to investigate MetaChem," I disagreed. "She's got more notes on that story, and Beth said that Kathy spent a lot of time hanging out around that place. They kicked her off the premises. They obviously had something to hide."

"Fine. We can do that. But it won't take long to rule out the Olde Tyme. All we have to do is sneak into the offices and snoop around a little, make sure it's all on the level."

"You just want to stay in the hotel tonight," I told him.

"Well, yeah." Joe's face broke into a huge grin. "This place has a roller coaster, did you know that? On the *roof*!"

That did sound cool. "Fine," I said. "It's too late to do anything else tonight, anyway. But first thing in the morning, we head over to MetaChem. Kathy's time is running out."

JOE

5.

Under the Casino

The clatter of a room service cart out in the hallway
woke me up good and early the next morning. I sat
up and stretched, ready for the day. Frank will tell
you that I sleep late, but that's only when we're not
on a mission. If I've got cool stuff to do, I don't like
to waste my time in dreamland. That's more than
you can say for my brother, though. Frank was still
fast asleep in the other bed.

Should I wake him up? I wondered.

I tossed a pillow at him. Frank just turned over
and kept on snoring.

I jumped out of bed and quickly got dressed. No
point in me wasting time just because Frank was
lazy. I'd go downstairs and check out the casino
offices, just to see if I could find any evidence of . . .

well, of *anything* weird. Kathy's notes hadn't said much about the Olde Tyme. But if she had spotted something weird after coming here one time with Tony, I should be able to spot the same thing.

Frank was still out cold when I left, pocketing one of the two key cards. I jogged down the hallway and took a glass-walled elevator to the ground floor. The sounds from the casino were just as loud as they had been the night before. In fact, the whole place seemed exactly the same in the morning as it had at night. There were no windows, so no sunlight got inside. The same music was playing over the speaker system, and the gambling machines were making all the same little beeps and dings and whirs. The only way I could tell it was daytime was that there weren't as many people in the place. The blackjack table where Tony had played was empty: no cards, no chips, not even a dealer. Most of the roulette wheels weren't spinning, and I only saw two poker games going on.

I headed for the slot machines. Kathy's notes had said something about rigged slots, so that seemed like a good place to start. Two old ladies were sitting side by side, chatting while they fed nickels into the machines.

"Excuse me," I said. "Do you mind if I ask you a question?"

"That depends on the question, sweetheart," one of the ladies replied. The other one laughed. I laughed too.

"I was just wondering if anybody ever wins at these things," I said. "The slot machines."

The two ladies exchanged a look, and the first one pursed her lips. "I've won some money from slots from time to time," she said. "Nothing big, of course. Just the occasional little jackpot."

"But not here," the other lady muttered.

"I haven't seen anybody win at this casino," the first one said. "It's new, though."

"The Olde Tyme is new?" I asked, surprised.

"It's only been here for a couple of years," the first lady answered. "Could be it takes time for the slots to start paying out. And we're not here all the time, of course."

"I'm sure people win sometimes," her friend added. "We just haven't seen it ourselves."

"Why do you come if you never win?" I asked, confused. "Do you also play roulette or something else?"

The ladies laughed. "No, sweetheart, that's too rich for my blood," the first one said. "I'll stick with the nickel slots."

"We like the feel of the place, and we like these old machines," the other lady added. "You go to

Atlantic City these days, and all the slot machines are just big computers. I like feeling the wheels actually spin."

"Are these slot machines old?" I asked, studying them. "But the rest of the place is new?"

"They're antique," the first lady told me. "It goes with the theme. Old times."

I had been checking things out while the women talked. There were a few other people playing slots, most of them senior citizens like these two. Nothing looked out of the ordinary. Maybe Frank was right and there was no story here. Kathy could've just decided to stop working on her Tony article and that's why she never spoke to him again.

The big security guard from the day before walked past our aisle, and I quickly turned away. I wasn't supposed to be in the casino. When we'd registered as hotel guests the night before, the man at the desk had made it clear that we were allowed in the lobby and the restaurants and stuff, but absolutely not in the casino. If this guard caught me, that would be the end of our investigation. It wasn't much of an investigation, but I still wanted to check out the casino office. They had to have reports of slot machine winnings. I would make sure that somebody won occasionally, just to confirm the old ladies' assumption.

"Have a nice day," I told the two women. Then I walked off—in the opposite direction from Gigantor.

I had seen enough heist movies to know that casinos keep their offices underground, with the vault where all the money goes. That meant I had to get down there . . . but how?

I spotted an elevator near the shops. It wasn't one of the glass-walled hotel ones, so it must have been a service elevator. Lettering on the door read RESTRICTED AREA. The closest shop was the kind of place that my girl friends always love—it sold candles, and little sparkly things that you hang in the window, and all that kind of stuff. I took a deep breath and stepped inside. The place smelled like a fruit salad.

"Can I help you?" asked the woman at the counter.

"Uh, no thanks," I said. "I'm just looking."

And I was—I was looking at the elevator. I hung out near a display of small china elephants, pretending to examine each one as if I were trying to make a decision. But really I was watching as a security guard walked up to the service elevator. He flipped open a small hatch on the wall and punched in a number. Then he passed an ID badge over it. The doors opened.

Score, I thought. I hadn't noticed the panel on the wall. It was pretty well hidden.

When some guy in a suit stopped at the elevator and flipped open the hatch, I stepped closer to the window of the shop so I could see better. He punched in a 2, then an 8.

"I'd be happy to help you pick something out," the saleswoman said, sounding irritated.

"Sorry," I said, giving her a smile. "My mother has a ton of elephant figurines, so I have to make sure I don't buy a repeat."

"I see," she said sourly. She went back to dusting something on another shelf, and I went back to casing the elevator. She had interrupted me before I could get the whole code. Luckily, a dealer from the casino came up a few moments later, carrying a tray of chips. He flipped open the panel and hit a 2, then an 8, then two 1s and a 5. He passed his ID badge over the sensor and went into the elevator.

"Got it!" I whispered. Now that I knew the code, all I needed was a badge and I was in. "I think my mom has all these. Thanks, anyway," I told the saleswoman. She frowned at me as I headed back out into the hallway. A couple of security dudes were coming my way. As long as I wasn't in the casino, I didn't have to avoid them.

"Excuse me," I said. "Do you know the way to the roller coaster?"

"Just go up to the top floor and follow the

signs," the short one said, barely even looking at me. Good thing too, because he didn't notice me unhooking the ID badge from his belt.

"Thanks."

I waited until they had passed the shops and turned the corner toward the health club before I sauntered over to the elevator . . . and kept right on sauntering. The woman from the candle store was watching me like a hawk. Obviously I was going to need a disguise. I wandered back toward the main lobby and the casino. I couldn't exactly score a security guard uniform, but maybe I could lift a visor from one of the dealers.

Better yet, maybe I can hide behind a janitor's cart, I thought as a guy in a white jumpsuit pushed his cleaning cart out of a ladies' room door in front of me. Nobody looks at janitors. The snooty saleswoman would never notice me if I had the cart. I bent down and pretended to tie my shoe, keeping an eye on the janitor the whole time. He grabbed a mop and a bucket, stuck a CLOSED FOR CLEANING sign on the men's room door, and pushed the bucket inside. Perfect!

I straightened up and started walking—right toward the cart. Without missing a step, I grabbed the cart and kept going, wheeling it in front of me. *Just take your time mopping in there, buddy,* I told the janitor silently. If he came out and saw me with his supplies, I was in trouble.

I picked up speed, heading for the service elevator. There was a baseball cap hung over a spray bottle full of some blue liquid on the top of the cart. I grabbed the cap and stuck it on my head. Keeping my back to the candle shop, I stopped at the elevator and flipped open the panel on the wall.

"Two, eight, one, one, five," I whispered, punching in the numbers. I pulled the guard's ID badge out of my pocket and swiped it over the sensor. The elevator doors opened just as another dealer came walking up. She glanced at me, and I caught my breath. Did she know I didn't work here?

"Excuse me," she said, slipping past the cart and into the elevator.

"No problem." I pushed the cart in and stepped inside, making sure not to look at her for too long. She didn't seem to have noticed much about me, and I didn't want to make more of an impression on her. The elevator took us down what felt like a floor or two, then the doors opened with a *ding!*

I pushed the cart out and paused. The dealer went to the right, so I turned left. With the cap pulled way down over my eyes, I could keep people from seeing my face. But I wasn't dressed in the hotel uniform, so I was pretty out of place. I had to find a hiding spot in a hurry. But where?

The hallway I found myself in was narrow and lit with bright fluorescent bulbs. Unmarked doorways lined both sides. Olde Tyme workers walked by—some dealers, some just people in suits. I followed a woman in a suit for a while, hoping she would lead me to the main hotel offices. But she just turned into a little kitchen and started pouring coffee. I reached an intersection and turned left into another hall. This place was huge!

The crackle of walkie-talkie static caught my attention, and I slowed down. A set of double doors on my left stood open, and the sound came from inside. As I inched past, I took a look inside. A bank of monitors met my gaze, along with a few uniform security people sitting there watching them. The entire place must have been rigged with cameras, and they all led to these monitors.

It wasn't the main office, but it was obviously the main security center for the Olde Tyme. That could be even better. Besides, I was tired of pushing the stupid cart around, and the janitor must have noticed it was gone by now. It was time to disappear.

Up ahead was another intersection. I strolled to the corner, pushed the cart around it, and stopped. The new hall was empty. Good. I gave the cart a push, tossed the baseball cap after it, then ran in the other direction, back toward the security center. A quick glance into the room showed me that the people inside all had their backs to the door, so I darted inside and immediately dove to the ground.

On the way past, I'd noticed a desk pushed right up against the doorway. There was a computer on it, but nobody was sitting there. I slid underneath and pressed my back against the far wall. In order to see me, the security guards would have to get down on the floor and look under the desk.

Now I'll just do some recon, I thought. *Maybe the guards will talk about the slot machines. And if not, I'll just have to find a way to get a look at the monitors that show them.*

If Kathy had discovered a story here, I would find out what it was. I was in the perfect position for snooping. The guards had no idea I was there.

And then my cell phone rang.

6.

Chemical Reaction

"Pick up, pick up, pick up," I muttered into my cell phone.

"Hello?"

"Joe, where are—"

"Gotcha! Joe's not available right now. You know what to do," my brother's annoying voice mail message went on.

"You could've left me a note," I said after the beep. "I don't know where you are. Call me back." I hit end and sighed. It was just like Joe to take off without bothering to tell me. The only surprising part about it was that he had woken up so early.

I glanced at the brochure for the Olde Tyme Resort and Casino. Right on the front cover was a photo of the rooftop roller coaster, a gleaming, twisting thing of beauty with cars that were supposed to look like old-fashioned streetcars. I really wanted to try it out—and I had a pretty strong feeling that Joe did too. He was probably up there right now, racing around the tracks.

"No fun until Kathy's safe," I said out loud. Kathy Boutry had been gone for almost two days now. We had to find her soon, before her captors did something stupid. There was no time to waste, which meant that I was just going to have to get on with the investigation whether Joe was here or not.

I grabbed the hotel phone and dialed home. Luckily, Dad answered. "Hang on while I close the door, Frank," he said, his voice hushed. Dad is the only one in the family who knows that Joe and I work for ATAC, because he's the one who recruited us! After he retired from the police force, he helped found American Teens Against Crime. I don't know how we would keep the whole thing secret from Mom and Aunt Trudy without Dad around to run interference. "Okay, now we can talk," he said when he returned. "Your mother is downstairs, and even Trudy can't hear through the bedroom door."

"What did you tell them, anyway?" I asked.

"That you boys were off working on a story for the back-to-school issue of your high school newspaper," he said. "Your adviser at school is a friend of ATAC, so she'll back us up."

"Really? Mrs. Rosa?" I was surprised. The woman had always seemed so boring. I guess we're not the only ones with a secret life!

"So how are things going, Frank?" Dad asked.

"Not so good," I admitted. "Our first lead turned out to be a dead end."

"I'm sorry to hear that. What will you do now?"

"We need to check out a chemical company that Kathy was investigating," I said. I figured I'd leave out the part about Joe being AWOL. I didn't want to get him in trouble. He would probably turn up by the time I finished talking to Dad, anyway. "That's why I'm calling. Can you look up the place for me? It's called MetaChem. Kathy has the name of the CEO, but nothing else."

I heard Dad typing away on his keyboard, logging into the restricted files ATAC keeps on all sorts of things. "MetaChem . . . they do chemical manufacturing, mostly polyurethane and nylon. Plus some research into newer production methods. It's a fairly small company, but a big moneymaker."

"Kathy thought they might be dumping illegally," I told him. "We're going to follow her story and hope it leads us to her."

"Hmm. This doesn't sound much like an ATAC

mission anymore," Dad said. "I'm not sure I like the idea of you two tangling with this place, especially if they've already taken one hostage."

"We'll be fine," I said quickly. "Joe and I can take care of ourselves." I was not about to get taken off this case. Kathy was missing, and we were going to find her. Period.

"I know, I know," Dad said. Even though he wants us in ATAC, he still worries a lot. "Just be careful. I'm going to send you the info I have on MetaChem."

My PDA beeped, letting me know Dad's files had arrived. "Thanks," I said. "We'll check in later."

"Okay," Dad said before he hung up. "Say hi to Joe for me."

I would if I knew where he was, I thought. But Joe wasn't back yet. Well, too bad. I couldn't wait any longer—he'd just have to catch up to me. I grabbed the hotel notepad next to the phone and scrawled: "J—Meet me at noon for lunch. Lobby restaurant. F."

Then I was out the door.

When I got down to the garage, the first thing I did was beam MetaChem's address from my PDA to the GPS device on my motorcycle. The small screen immediately opened a map showing the fastest route. Even so, it would take twenty minutes to get there. I hopped on, revved the engine, and took off.

Twenty minutes of riding my supercool bike? No problem!

When I got to MetaChem, I slowed down to check the place out. It was a low office building, only one floor. But it spread out pretty far in either direction, and there was a tall, chain-link fence around an outdoor section to the back, with all kinds of machinery inside the fence. I drove my motorcycle into the narrow roadway that snaked around behind the machine section, pulled to the curb, and climbed off. From here, the fenced area blocked my view of the parking lot. Hopefully it would also block me from view. I knew there had to be security nearby—Kathy's roommate had told us so.

I shot a quick glance around. The coast was clear. I grabbed hold of the fence as high as I could reach over my head and pulled myself up. It was a quick climb to the top, then I swung my legs over, eased down until I was dangling from my finger-tips, and let go. I dropped to the ground and rolled right up.

The machines looked bigger up close. I had no idea what they were doing, but the whole place smelled like some kind of oil. The two machines closest to me were giving out a low, vibrating hum, and the air around them felt charged. *Magnets,* I thought. I had been given an MRI once when I broke my arm on an ATAC mission (well, Mom thought I broke it by falling off my mountain bike—as if I ever fall off!). In the MRI room, you could actually *feel* the magnets in the big machine. That's what it felt like here.

The hair on my arms stood on end as I squeezed in between the two machines. Behind them was a tall, thin machine with three hatches on the front. A huge biohazard sign was painted along the top.

I stopped in my tracks. I was not about to go anywhere near that thing. I took a step backward, then another, then I circled around to take a look at the last machine. This one was just a big black box that gave off a series of clicks every thirty seconds.

"Great," I murmured. "Now I know . . . exactly as much as I knew before." These machines didn't look like anything I had ever seen. How was I supposed to know what they were doing? None of them seemed to be leaking hazardous waste into the ground or anything. Did Kathy Boutry know what these things were? Was there more stuff like this inside MetaChem?

Suddenly an unmistakable sound reached me. An engine giving off a low whine. I knew it wasn't a car, and it wasn't a motorcycle. *Golf cart,* I thought. The kind of golf cart that security guards use to patrol.

I grabbed the lip of the black box machine and hoisted myself up to get a better look. Over the top of the box I could see a black and white cart moving slowly through the parking lot. Inside was a tall, dark-haired guy wearing a uniform. Definitely a security guard. And definitely a security guard who would collar me if he found me in here with the huge machinery.

The cart crept along the first line of cars, heading toward the corner that led to the fenced area. I had to get back to my bike before the guard saw it parked there. If he found the bike, he'd know I was here.

I raced toward the magnetic machines, turning sideways to edge between them. Then I sprinted to the fence, jumped into the air, and grabbed for the top. If I didn't make it, I wouldn't be able to get over fast enough.

Got it! My hands grasped the cold metal of the top bar. I slammed my feet against the fence, ignoring the loud rattle it made. Moving fast, I pushed away and used the thrust to kick my feet out behind me. At the same time, I straightened my arms and locked my elbows to support my full weight.

For one split second I was upside down, doing a handstand on the very top of the fence. Then the momentum carried my legs down over the other side. As soon as my sneakers were lower than my hands, I let go and flipped through the air. I landed on my feet, facing away from the fence.

No time to waste. I sped for my bike, leapt on, revved it, and took off down the stretch of blacktop just as the security cart came around the corner behind me.

Had he seen me? There was no way to tell. I kept driving, all the way around the back of the building and back to the parking lot in front. I slowed, waiting for the guy on the golf cart to show up. From here, I could take off out onto the street without him getting a look at my license plate. But ten seconds went by. Twenty. I relaxed. The golf cart hadn't come after me.

He hadn't seen me.

I parked in the lot. It was time to check out the CEO Kathy had mentioned in her notes. I shoved open the glass door to the building and headed inside.

I don't know what I was expecting from a chemical manufacturing headquarters. Probably people in lab coats and little cages full of rats and tables covered with beakers holding mystery substances.

What I didn't expect was a totally boring, totally typical office. The kind with ugly gray carpeting and people in business suits working on computers or talking on the phone.

Where were the researchers? How could these people do all that chemical stuff Dad had mentioned without microscopes and petri dishes?

I gazed around the big open space, checking out the cubicles and the bored-looking workers. What kind of story had Kathy found here?

"Help ya?" a squeaky voice asked. I turned to see a big desk against the wall next to the door. A cute girl with curly red hair was sitting behind it, a telephone headset looped over her hair. She raised her eyebrows at me. "Hello?"

"Uh, hi," I said. "I didn't know you were talking to me."

She suddenly pulled the headset microphone forward and said, "MetaChem, please hold." Then she shoved it to the side and grinned at me. "So who are you?"

I took a deep breath and tried to stop the blush from working its way up my cheeks. No good. I just can't talk to girls without being embarrassed. "Frank," I said.

Her smile grew wider. "Frank, huh? Just Frank?"

"Oh! No. I'm Frank Hardy. Sorry," I stammered.

"You're sorry you're Frank Hardy?" she teased.

"No. I mean—"

"I'm just playing," she cut in. "My name is Lucy Lopez, but you can call me Lou."

"Lou," I repeated.

She rolled her eyes. "I know—it's a truck driver's name, right? That's what my mother is always telling me." The phone on her desk rang, and she pulled the headset microphone forward again. "MetaChem, please hold." She looked up at me. "But I think it has personality, don't you?"

"Excuse me?" I asked, confused.

"Wow, you're really polite," Lucy told me. "Personality. Don't you think Lou is better than Lucy?"

I opened my mouth, then closed it again. How was I supposed to answer that? "Don't you have two people on hold?" I asked.

"Yeah." She shrugged. "I'd rather talk to you than to *them*. You're cuter."

My cheeks had felt hot before, but now they felt as if they were going to burst into flame. How does Joe do it? He would be flirting right back, but I couldn't even make myself look Lucy in the eye. "You don't know what they look like," I pointed out.

She laughed. "That's true. But I know what *you* look like. Are you a scientist?"

"Huh?" I said stupidly.

"A researcher?" Lucy asked. "Or are you here to sell us something?"

"Oh. No. I'm . . . uh . . . I'm working on a story. For the school paper. About MetaChem," I mumbled.

"Cool. You want a copy of the press packet?" Lucy slid a shiny folder across the table to me. The phone rang again, and she rolled her eyes.

"I'd better let you get back to work," I started.

Lucy held up a finger to silence me. "Meta-Chem, please hold," she said again. "So what else can I do for you, Frank Hardy?"

"Um . . . I was hoping I could talk to Saul Gold," I replied. It was the only name Kathy had written in her notebook.

Lucy raised her eyebrows. "The boss, huh? One sec." She pushed a button on the phone and said, "Sollie? Frank Hardy for you."

"He's not expecting me," I said quickly.

"You can go on in, anyway." Lucy gave me a wink. "This office right here." She gestured to a closed door about five feet away.

"Thanks." I didn't think Sollie was going to be too thrilled to see me, but I wasn't about to wait until he refused to let me in. I pushed open the door and walked in just as the guy at the desk was busy saying, "I'm not available" through the intercom.

I guess Lucy doesn't care if he's available or not, I thought with a smile.

"This will only take a minute, Mr. Gold," I told him.

The guy looked me up and down, and I looked right back. He was a huge dude with a mean face and a military-style crew cut. But he was more overweight than muscular, and I wasn't worried. If he had kidnapped Kathy, I could kick his butt.

SUSPECT PROFILE

<u>Name:</u> Saul "Sollie" Gold

<u>Hometown:</u> Monroe, NJ

<u>Physical description:</u> Age 56, 6'1", 250 lbs., Dark eyes, short gray hair

<u>Occupation:</u> CEO of MetaChem, Inc., a chemical manufacturing and research company

<u>Background:</u> PhD from Stanford, MBA from Harvard Business School; divorced

<u>Suspicious behavior:</u> Had security throw Kathy Boutry off MetaChem premises; fired Kathy from her temp job at MetaChem

<u>Suspected of:</u> Illegal dumping; kidnapping Kathy Boutry

<u>Possible motive:</u> Wants to prevent word of his company's illegal activities from reaching the media

"Who are you?" Sollie Gold asked.

"Frank Hardy. I'm Kathy Boutry's assistant," I lied.

"Who?" He frowned at me.

"Kathy Boutry. I'm here to follow up on the dumping story she filed with the *Press of Atlantic City*." I knew Kathy hadn't actually filed a story, or even written one. But it was the best way to get Sollie to pay attention. If he thought Kathy had already turned in the story, he would realize there was no reason to hold her hostage. He'd think that whatever damage she could do to MetaChem had already been done.

"Dumping?" he demanded. "What are you talking about?"

"Illegal dumping of toxic waste," I replied. "I only need a few minutes of your time, Mr. Gold."

"You think I'm gonna talk to you?" he bellowed. "You think I'm about to let you publish a bunch of lies about my company?"

"I'm only here to check the facts," I told him. "Kathy Boutry is the one who—"

"Out!" He pointed to the door. "Get out of my office. Get out of my building. Right. Now." The guy had turned almost purple from his crew cut all the way down his face. He was majorly angry. Angry enough to hurt Kathy?

I may leave, I told him silently, *but I'll be sticking around to watch where you go next. If you go to Kathy, I'll be following.*

"We'll print the story, anyway," I told him as I turned to go.

Saul Gold didn't answer. He had already snatched up his phone and started yelling into it. "Lou, I want the *Press of Atlantic City* on the line. Immediately. The editor in chief."

Outside the office, I paused by Lucy's desk and waited for her to stop dialing the phone. She glanced up at me with a smile. "What did you say to him?" she asked, her eyes brimming with curiosity.

"I guess I asked a question he didn't want to answer," I told her.

"Well, you *are* a reporter," she said. "I think he's talking to your boss at the paper."

"Can you listen in?" I asked.

"Ooh, naughty boy," she teased. "Don't tell anyone." She pushed a button on the phone, then handed me her headset.

I held it up to my ear. ". . . tell that Boutry girl to stay out of my business!" Sollie was yelling.

"Sir," said the newspaper editor, "I don't know—"

"I've had enough of her snooping around," Sollie interrupted. "I'll get a restraining order if I need one, against her and against any other reporter you send nosing around—"

He kept talking, but I stopped listening. A restraining order? That didn't make sense. None of it made sense. If Sollie wanted the paper to keep Kathy away from him, if he was thinking of getting a restraining order to keep her away . . . then it meant he still thought she was a threat to him.

He didn't know she was missing.

He wasn't the one who had kidnapped her.

7.

Ghost in the Machine

"Time to go," I whispered.

I inched out from under the desk, where I had been hiding for more than an hour. The office was dark and empty—a total stroke of luck. When my cell phone rang, I hadn't had time to think. I just chucked it away from me, sending it skidding across the floor of the security center while it kept on ringing. Then I ran the other way, out the door, into the hall, and through the very first door I came to—this empty office.

Had the security guards seen me? It was impossible to tell. I had gotten a quick glimpse of one of them watching the phone as it slid across the tile. Maybe all the others had watched the phone too.

Anyway, they hadn't come after me fast enough to see me duck in here.

But I had heard their boots slapping on the floor as they ran out two seconds later. I had heard them shouting to one another, and I had heard their walkie-talkies beeping and crackling with static as they reported back about their search for the intruder. For me.

I grinned, remembering it. It was kinda like being in an action movie, with everybody searching for the hero.

Still, the whole thing was starting to get a little old. I'd been hiding in here for ages, my legs had cramped up from being squashed under the desk, and I hadn't managed to find out anything about Kathy Boutry's story.

There hadn't been any noise out in the hallway for the past ten minutes or so. It was a good time to leave. I took a quick look around the office. When I'd run inside, I locked the door, dove straight under the desk, and stayed there. Nobody had even tried the knob, but I stayed hidden, anyway . . . until now.

I didn't turn on any lights, but I could see well enough by the light coming in under the crack of the door. The place was posh. The desk hadn't seemed very big from underneath, but now that I got a good look at it, I could see that it was pretty huge and was made of some kind of gleaming, polished wood. A marble nameplate stood along the front, with the name DOMINIC ASHER engraved on it. Two big couches were set up to one side, and a couple of leather chairs faced the desk. Some kind of abstract painting glared at me from the wall. No doubt about it: This was the office of a VIP. No wonder the guards hadn't dared to come inside.

Good thing the honcho isn't here today, I thought as I tiptoed over to the door. I unlocked it and opened it a tiny crack.

The first thing I saw was Gigantor. He stood against the wall right next to me, less than five feet away. I shut the door and gulped in a breath. That was close! If he'd been turned in my direction, he would've seen me for sure.

He's standing outside the security center, I realized. *They must have put an extra guard on to deal with the intruder.*

Well, I couldn't go that way. I chewed my lip, thinking it over. The hallway was blocked, and this office had no windows, being underground and all. There was only one other way out: up.

There was a golf bag in the corner. I grabbed a putter and climbed onto the shiny desk, careful not to step on any of the neat piles of paper. I held the putter over my head and poked at the ceiling. The whole thing lifted right up. It was a flimsy tile job, like the ceilings we have in Bayport High. There was no way it would hold my weight.

My gaze fell on a vent in the wall. It was eye level with me as I stood on the desk. And it looked big enough to climb through. "Perfect," I murmured. I made my way over to the edge of the desk and reached up, yanking the metal grating off the wall. I slid the grate inside the air duct. It wasn't easy to get a handhold. I had to jump up and grab the edge of the vent. The metal at the edge tore my fingertips, but I held on, anyway

I tugged myself up and into the air vent. It was a tight fit. The vent was wide enough, but I couldn't get up on my hands and knees without banging my head against the top. *No problem,* I thought. *I'm only going one room over.*

I replaced the metal grate over the vent, then crawled along the duct on my stomach, combat-style. Since the posh office was right next door to the security center, I figured the next vent I came to would lead to that room. Then I could check out the monitors and see if I could spot anything strange going on.

A bluish light cut through the vent up ahead. I crawled over to it and pressed my eye to the slats in the vent. Through it I could see a bank of security monitors showing various hotel hallways and the reception desk.

"Well, that's not helpful," I muttered. But the room was big. There had to be more than one air vent. I crawled farther down the duct until I found another vent. *Score.* From this vent I could see a different set of monitors. These were showing the casino. I could just settle back and watch the slot machines for any signs of weirdness. Kathy's notes had mentioned rigged slots, but I wasn't entirely sure what that meant. Still, if the slot machines were rigged, they would probably do something odd. I'd watch them and see.

Below me, one of the security guards put his feet up on the desk in front of the wall of monitors. The other guard, a woman, yawned and stretched.

"What time is The Boss getting here?" the guy asked.

"Who knows?" the woman replied. "He does what he wants. Good thing he wasn't here this morning, though."

The dude whistled. "No kidding. He would've lost it with that thief running around."

"He'll still lose it when he finds out that we haven't caught the guy," the woman said. "I wouldn't be surprised if he fires us all."

"Why? It's no big deal," the guy insisted. "He didn't get anywhere near the vault, and now we've got extra muscle on."

The female guard snorted. "He was obviously just testing us to find our weak spots," she said. "He'll come back another time for the money. You think The Boss won't realize that?"

I felt a smile break across my face. I'd really freaked them out. They thought I was here to plan a casino heist! Cool.

"You don't know Asher like I do," she went on. "He's got a temper. Once he fired a poker dealer just for wearing a vest with a rip in it."

Asher, I thought. My mind flashed back to the nameplate on the desk next door. *Dominic Asher.* That's who had the gigantic office. Dominic Asher, The Boss.

"I heard he was an ex-con," the security guy said. "And that he did five years for murder."

The woman shook her head. "He did six months in jail for assault. Not murder. And it was a long time ago, before he owned the casino."

"Still," the guy replied. "Assault is pretty bad—he must have a bad temper. Maybe you're right about him. Maybe he is gonna be mad enough to fire us all."

Yeah, I thought. *And maybe he was mad enough to kidnap Kathy Boutry.*

SUSPECT PROFILE

<u>Name:</u> Dominic Asher

<u>Hometown:</u> Hoboken, NJ

<u>Physical description:</u> Age 31, 6'2", 200 lbs., muscular

<u>Occupation:</u> Owner of the Olde Tyme Resort and Casino

<u>Background:</u> Spent six months in jail for assault; bought the Olde Tyme Restaurant and expanded it to a theme hotel and casino

<u>Suspicious behavior:</u> Short temper

<u>Suspected of:</u> Rigging slot machines, kidnapping Kathy Boutry

<u>Possible motive:</u> To prevent Kathy from writing an exposé about the rigged slot machines at the Olde Tyme Resort and Casino

8.

Brother's Keeper

"Are you sure you don't want to order?" the waiter asked me, an annoyed expression on his face.

"No, thanks, I'm going to wait for my brother," I told him.

The guy sighed, fiddling with the bow tie on his uniform. "You've been waiting for half an hour, and it's the lunch rush," he said. "I can't let you sit here any longer without ordering."

I glanced around the restaurant. It was situated in the heart of the huge lobby area of the hotel, and it was obviously the most popular place to eat. Every table was full, and there was a line at the hostess stand. "Okay," I told the waiter. "Never mind."

"Thanks," he called after me as I got up and left. My stomach gave a rumble as I walked back out into the lobby. It was twelve thirty and Joe still wasn't here. Normally I would be angry if he was that late. But now I was starting to get worried. It wasn't like Joe to be late for food. Maybe he hadn't found my note saying to meet me.

I pulled out my cell and hit Joe's speed-dial number. He'd been AWOL all morning.

"Hello?" a voice answered. A gruff, deep voice.

Not Joe's voice.

I hung up immediately, my heart pounding in my chest. Why was some other dude answering my brother's phone? Where was Joe?

My cell phone rang. I checked the number—Joe's phone.

"I'm not that stupid," I muttered, hitting end. Obviously whoever had Joe's phone wanted to know who was calling him. But if they knew who I was, I might be in danger too. A moment later, the phone rang again.

I looked at the screen. It was a different number this time. But it seemed familiar somehow: 609-555-0221.

The registration desk was nearby. I jogged over and snagged a hotel pen. There was a phone number printed on the side: 609-555-0200.

"It's the same general number," I murmured. Whoever was calling me was right here, in the Olde

Tyme Resort and Casino. And it seemed pretty clear that he had Joe's cell phone. What was going on?

Where was my brother?

What had happened to Joe?

A slot machine about twenty feet away gave off a loud clicking sound as the wheels spun around—and suddenly I knew exactly what had happened. Joe thought the slot machines were rigged, he had said so last night. He thought that was the story Kathy was working on.

He decided to check out the casino himself, I thought. A wave of annoyance passed through me. Why did my brother have to be so impulsive all the time? Why couldn't he just stick to a plan? I pushed the thoughts away. The truth was, I was more worried than angry. Joe might be impulsive, but he was also good. If he was investigating the Olde Tyme and he'd been missing all morning, it could only mean one thing. It meant something had gone wrong.

I ran straight to the elevator and headed up to our room. I had left Kathy's notepad there, and I wanted to see what she'd said about this place. But even though I flipped through the whole thing, I couldn't find anything more than the few words she'd scribbled about rigged slots.

Think, I ordered myself. My brother was missing, and I had to find him. That's why there are two of us—we always watch each other's back. If Joe was trying to follow the trail of Kathy's casino article, then I had to do the same thing. That way, I would be following Joe's trail as well.

"She had to have more on this story," I said aloud, just the way I would have if Joe were in the room with me. "Maybe she had another notepad?"

Lame, a voice in my head replied. It sounded suspiciously like Joe's.

"Okay, not another notepad," I went on, beginning to pace the length of the hotel room. "But she couldn't have brought a notepad into the casino, anyway. It would be too obvious if she was sitting there talking to customers and taking notes, and Kathy is an experienced reporter. She wouldn't do that."

So she used something else, my inner Joe replied. *A tape recorder or something.*

"So where is it?" I wondered. "When she was kidnapped, did she have it with her? Did she leave it in her dorm room? Did she leave it in the car?"

I stopped walking. The car! My brain was whirling. We had come to the casino from Kathy's college, and it was kind of a hike. She couldn't have walked, and it didn't seem likely that Beth or anyone would have been too thrilled about driving her all the way here just to work on yet another article. She must have driven herself.

So where was her car?

I grabbed my cell and dialed the number for Vijay Patel. He's another teen who works for ATAC. He answered on the first ring. "Frank?"

"Hey, Vijay," I said. "I need your help."

"Absolutely. Anything I can do, anything at all," Vijay said eagerly. He wants to be a field agent, so he has a little bit of hero worship for Joe and me. But his job is totally cool too. He's the one who brings us our assignments half the time, and he always seems to know what's going on in all the different ATAC cases. Vijay was hooked in, and that's what I needed right now.

"There's one thing, though," I told him. "You can't tell anyone at ATAC about this. I don't want my father to worry."

"Oh . . . okay, I guess," Vijay said slowly. "Worry about what?"

"Joe's missing."

Vijay gasped.

"I'm going to find him," I assured him. "I just need your help. I'm looking for a car. It belongs to Kathy Boutry."

"The kidnapped reporter," Vijay said. "ATAC traced her car as soon as the case came in. It was at a mechanic's shop. Apparently she had crashed it two weeks ago and it was still getting fixed."

"She crashed her car?" I asked, frowning. "I wonder if that has anything to do with her being kidnapped. Maybe someone was following her or trying to ram her or something. Maybe whoever hit her was the same person who nabbed her."

"I doubt it," Vijay said. "Unless she was kidnapped by Bambi."

"Huh?"

"The accident report says Kathy was driving out near Hammonton Lake State Park when a deer ran into the road. Kathy swerved to avoid it, and hit a guardrail."

"Oh." I was disappointed. "I guess I can't use her car as a lead, then. But she had to get around somehow. What was she using if her car was in the shop?"

"Maybe she rented a car?" Vijay suggested.

"No, she's too young to rent one," I replied. "But maybe she borrowed one! Who would lend her a car?"

"Her mom or dad, probably," Vijay said. "But ATAC's mission report says that her parents are on a cruise to Alaska this week. Since Kathy hasn't been officially reported to the cops as a missing person yet, her parents haven't been informed. When she's been gone for two days, the police will alert them. But we're all hoping you guys find her before then."

"Yeah, I'm hoping that too," I said. "So, she could be borrowing her parents' car since they're away, right?"

"I guess so," Vijay said. "The ATAC files say that her mother's name is Penelope Boutry."

"Great. Can you check to see if she has a car?"

"I'm on it." I heard him tapping away at his computer. "Okay, I've got the license plate number from the DMV records. There's only one car. Although there's another one registered under her father's name, Max Boutry."

"Well, it's worth a shot. Can you run those plates through the police database?" I asked. "If somebody found her car, it could be at an impound lot or something."

Vijay was silent for a moment, and I heard his keyboard in action. "Nope," he finally replied. "I'm using the ATAC system to check the New Jersey State Troopers as well as the local police, but her mother's plate isn't coming up anywhere. Neither is her father's plate."

"Bummer," I muttered. I'd really been hoping I could find a lead that way.

"Wait, I think I have something better," Vijay said, excitement creeping into his voice. "Yes! Kathy's mother has a LoJack."

"A tracking device?" I asked.

"Yup. It's weird, though. . . ." Vijay's voice trailed off.

"What is?"

"Well, the device is showing Penelope's car at some kind of resort in New Jersey. But if her parents are supposed to be away . . . I guess Kathy wasn't borrowing it, after all. I mean, Kathy herself wouldn't be at a casino, she's a—"

"A casino?" I interrupted. "Is it the Olde Tyme Resort and Casino?"

"Yeah." Vijay sounded impressed. "How did you know that?"

"Lucky guess," I said ruefully.

"Um, do you want the address?"

"No, I'm already there," I told him.

"Wow," Vijay whispered. "That's unbelievable."

"It sure is," I murmured. I really couldn't believe it. I seriously doubted that Kathy's mother and father had flown back from Alaska just to come here, which meant that Kathy had probably borrowed the car and taken it to the Olde Tyme to investigate. And it was still here. My heart began to pound. It looked like Joe had been right, after all. The story was here, at the casino. "Listen, man, I gotta go. E-mail me that license plate number, okay?" I said to Vijay. "Thanks."

I was already on my way out the door. I took the stairs down to the lobby and went straight to the registration desk. "Hi, I'm looking for a guest here," I told the short guy behind the counter. "Kathy Boutry."

He looked her up in the computer. "I don't have anyone with that name," he said.

"Are you sure?" I asked. "I thought I saw her car in the garage."

He checked the computer again and shrugged. "I have no record of her."

Maybe Kathy never made it to the hotel, I thought. *Maybe she was kidnapped right from the casino.*

"Thanks." I jogged back over to the staircase and went down to the garage. Vijay had already sent me the plate number for Kathy's car, but I had no idea where it was parked. I'd have to look for it the old-fashioned way: I walked up and down the lines of cars until I finally found it, a new VW Beetle convertible.

The car was easy to get into, but it wasn't so easy to find anything useful inside. Kathy might be a great reporter, but she was also a slob! The Bug was filled with empty water bottles and food wrappers and textbooks. I sifted through the junk, looking for anything that might give me a clue as to where Kathy—and Joe—had been taken.

Finally, underneath a gym bag on the floor of the tiny backseat, I spotted a backpack. When I pulled it open, I found a glossy folder among the news magazines inside—a folder just like the one in my hotel room upstairs. It was an information folder for the Olde Tyme Resort and Casino. I flipped it open and glanced at the papers inside.

"Score," I whispered. Among the hotel maps and lists of amenities was a computer printout of customer complaints. Kathy must have talked one of the hotel workers into giving it to her. I ran my finger down the printout, looking for anything out of the ordinary.

A lot of it seemed pretty standard: complaints about hotel rooms being run-down, bathroom fixtures being broken, the service at the restaurant being too slow. But as I skimmed through, I noticed more and more complaints about the slot machines. People saying they didn't work, that nobody ever wins. Some people threatened to report the casino to the New Jersey Gaming Commission. Others just asked for their money back.

Every complaint had a name at the end. And on page three there was a star drawn next to one name, along with an address scrawled in the margin next to it. On page five there was another star and another address.

"Did you go visit these two, Kathy?" I asked. "I think I'll find out why."

The first name was Edna Williams. I stuffed the complaint list into my jacket pocket and jogged over to my motorcycle. I typed the address into my GPS and climbed onto the bike. As I peeled out, I felt a pang of worry. Joe's bike was still back there, parked by itself.

I had to find my brother.

Edna Williams lived only a few miles from the Olde Tyme. When I pulled the motorcycle into the parking lot of her building, I was surprised to see that it was a retirement home. A bright yellow sign over the door read SUNNY TOMORROWS SENIOR LIVING. I pulled out the complaint list and double-checked it. Edna's complaint was about the slot machines. She had filed a complaint two weeks ago and wanted a refund.

Inside, a nurse at the desk directed me to room 215.

When I knocked at the door, I was expecting a shrunken little old lady to answer. But Edna was as tall as me and looked strong and healthy.

"Mrs. Williams?" I asked. "My name is Frank Hardy."

"Well, hello, Frank." She gave me a firm hand-shake. "What can I do for you today?"

"I'm looking for somebody," I told her. "And I think you may be able to help me."

"I'll certainly try," Edna said with a smile.

"Thank you." I pulled the complaint list out of my pocket. "I got your name from a list of people who had made complaints about the Olde Tyme—"

"Who are you?" Edna demanded. Her voice suddenly sounded shrill—and frightened.

"Mrs. Williams, I'm—"

"You get away," she cried. "Stay away from me!"

She slammed the door in my face.

9.
Trapped!

My sneaker had a big black scuff mark on it. I'd never noticed that before. Of course, I'd never spent this much time staring at my sneakers before. Turns out, there's not much else to do when you're hiding in a bathroom stall.

Outside the stall, a security guard was coming closer.

I was standing on the toilet so my feet wouldn't show underneath the door. But if he pushed open the door ... well, that would be it.

I had to be ready for a fight.

Why didn't I just stay up in the air ducts? I thought. I had been safe up there. Nobody had so much as stuck their head through a vent to see if I was there. But I had been lurking in the ducts for ages, so long that I almost fell asleep while watching the security monitors of the slot machines.

At least I had learned one thing: Those two old ladies had been right. No one ever won at the slot machines. I'd been watching like a hawk, and none of the machines ever even spat back a couple of quarters. Bo-ring. I'd much rather play poker than sit there feeding money into a machine just to watch the wheels spin.

Finally I couldn't take it anymore. The guards below weren't talking, the monitors weren't showing anything useful, and my entire body felt like one big cramp from being squeezed into the ducts for so long. So I had crawled around in the ducts until I found what I wanted: a vent into the bathroom.

It had seemed like the perfect plan. The bathroom was empty, so no one would see me come down from the vent. Then I'd simply walk out as if I were just some typical worker using the can.

But, no. I'd barely even finished getting the vent grating back on when the door opened. I'd run into a stall and closed the door. The two guys near the sinks didn't even seem to realize I was there.

"What's with the extra goonage?" one had asked the other.

"Some intruder in the pit," his friend replied.

"Security wants to find him before The Boss gets here. They're looking everywhere."

So that was my first clue that the great bathroom escape wasn't going to be easy. I waited for the two dudes to leave, then I reached for the stall door. Thanks to them, I knew the security guards were still searching for me. I knew I had to be careful.

Which is why I stayed in the stall when the bathroom door started to swing open two seconds after the guys left.

And which is why I pulled my feet up onto the toilet just to be extra safe.

The distinctive crackle of walkie-talkie static filled the bathroom as soon as the new person stepped inside. That combined with the ugly black boots I could see under the stall door told me that this was a security guard. Even Frank's ugly boots weren't that ugly.

I can't believe they're searching the bathrooms, I thought. *Shouldn't they have a more high-tech way to catch thieves?*

The door of the stall next to me creaked open as the guard looked inside. I held my breath. My stall was locked. Maybe that would be enough. . . .

The black boots reached my stall. I heard the guard put his hand on the door, and it gave a little bit when he tried to push it open. But the lock held firm.

"Great," the guard muttered. He took a step away from the door, and I thought I was in the clear. But then I saw the black boots move back to the stall next to me. He went in.

Uh-oh, I thought. *He's gonna get on that toilet and look over the door to see if I'm in here.*

I had a moment of panic. Should I run? Should I jump the guy? How could I prevent him from calling for backup the second he saw me?

A loud blast of static shrieked through the air. "All units report. Repeat: All units report," a voice said through the walkie-talkie.

"Darn thing," the guard yelped. He must've turned the volume down, because the next time the voice spoke, I couldn't hear what it said.

The guard's walkie-talkie gave a little beep and he said, "East men's room clear." Then it beeped again. Other voices came through, reporting that they hadn't found me.

I stayed perfectly still as the guard turned and headed back toward the door. When it finally swung shut behind me, I gulped in a deep breath of air. Thank god the walkie-talkie had distracted him!

But I couldn't stay here any longer. He might remember the locked stall and come right back.

Besides, I obviously couldn't stay down in these hallways any longer. The whole security force was searching for me. It was only a matter of time until they found me. I'd done all the snooping I could do for now. The whole investigation went bust the minute my stupid cell phone rang in the security center.

I'm not sure there's anything to find here, anyway, I thought ruefully. All I'd learned was that the Olde Tyme's owner was an ex-con and that the slot machines were a boring game to play. Maybe Frank had been right. The MetaChem story was a better bet for finding Kathy. As soon as I got back upstairs, I would find my brother and we'd head off to check out the chemical company.

Frank is going to be pretty mad at me, I thought. I had been down here for hours. Hopefully he'd gone on with the MetaChem investigation on his own.

I got off the toilet and unlocked the stall door. Then I ran for the bathroom door. I pulled the door open the tiniest crack and took a look outside. The hallway was clear, no security. Nobody at all, in fact.

And twenty feet away, a beautiful sight: a door marked STAIRWAY.

I didn't give myself time to think. I just jerked

the door open and ran full-out for the stairs. The door came closer . . . closer . . . I was there. I hurled my shoulder against it.

It didn't budge.

"Come on, come on," I whispered, pushing on it. But the door wasn't moving.

A panel on the wall caught my eye. It was just like the one upstairs near the elevator. Of course— the stairs were locked just like the elevator. I grabbed the stolen ID badge from my pocket, punched in the code, and swiped the card.

The light blinked red.

"Okay, slow down," I told myself. I punched in the code again: 2-8-1-1-5. I swiped the ID badge.

The light blinked red.

And then I realized the truth. They had changed the code. They knew I had gotten down here, so they'd reprogrammed the security codes. The place was in lockdown.

I was trapped.

10.
Deadly Game

"Mrs. Williams?" I called, staring at the door two inches in front of my face. "Is something wrong?" Why had she slammed the door on me?

"You get out of here!" the old lady yelled from inside. "I'm calling Security!"

Her voice was frightened, and I felt bad. I hadn't meant to upset the poor woman. But I honestly had no idea what had set her off. "I'm sorry to bother you," I called, trying to sound as friendly as possible. "I need your help to find my brother. He's missing."

She didn't answer. I hoped that meant she was listening.

"I got your address from Kathy Boutry. Did she come to see you, Mrs. Williams?" I went on. "Can you tell me what you talked to Kathy about?"

"Security is on the way," Edna called back. "You leave now!"

"Okay, I'm going," I told her. I grabbed the complaint list from my pocket, ripped off a corner of one page, and quickly wrote my name and my cell number. "But please call me if you change your mind." I shoved the paper under her door. "Please, Mrs. Williams."

Edna didn't say anything, and I could hear heavy footsteps running up the steps. I headed toward them. The last thing I wanted to do was get in a fight with the security guards. I met the two middle-aged guys at the top of the stairs. "I'm the one you want," I told them. "I was talking to Edna Williams."

The guys exchanged confused looks. I guess they weren't used to people turning themselves in.

"You'll have to leave now," the first guard said. "We'll escort you out."

"Okay." I started downstairs with them on my heels.

"What kind of jerk upsets an old lady like that?" the other guard muttered, loud enough for me to hear.

"That's exactly what I'm wondering," I told him. We'd reached the ground floor. "I'll see myself out."

The guards followed me to the front door and watched me until I made it over to my motorcycle.

I stopped there and gazed back up at the retirement home. What kind of jerk had gotten Edna so upset? It wasn't me. She had freaked out when I mentioned the Olde Tyme. Why?

I looked down at the list of complaints in my hand. Kathy had written one other address. This one was next to the name Milton Lanning. "Okay, Milton Lanning," I said, pulling on my helmet. "Let's hope you're a little more helpful."

When I entered Milton's address into my onboard computer, the GPS balked. It couldn't give me specific directions to the place—it could only put me at the nearest crossroads.

Weird, I thought. But when I reached the crossroads, I could understand why the computer was baffled. This place was in the middle of nowhere! There were trees on all sides, and just a little one-lane road winding through them. It was pretty, but lonely.

I checked the address on the paper, then looked around. There wasn't a house—or even a building— to be seen. I wondered if Kathy ever managed to find this guy. The address was on Ulster Lane, so I drove forward along Ulster Lane. After about half a mile, I began thinking I should turn back.

And then I saw it.

Through the trees, maybe a hundred yards from the road. A trailer.

I turned my bike and drove up to the place. It was a mobile home, but it obviously hadn't been mobile in a long time. A few cinder blocks led up to the door like stairs, and there were bushes planted along the base of the trailer. An old Chevy pickup was parked nearby. It had a ton of rust spots and a bumper sticker that said I'D RATHER BE GAMBLING.

I got off my bike and went up to the door.

"Hello?" I called, knocking on the thin metal. "Mr. Lanning?"

Nobody answered.

I knocked again, but I didn't expect much. The whole place had a deserted feel. But this had to be the right place. It was the only home anywhere nearby. And his car was here, so Milton Lanning should be here too.

"Mr. Lanning?" I called again. "Milton?"

Nothing.

I hopped off the cinder blocks and circled around to the back of the trailer. There was a window open near the end, its screen hanging slightly off the window frame. *That will do,* I thought. I reached for the screen and took it down. Then I grabbed the frame and hoisted myself up and in through the window.

It was dark inside. I gave my eyes a moment to adjust. I was standing in the kitchenette. I could make out a hot plate on the counter. A small sink with some dirty dishes piled inside.

A body on the floor.

It was Milton Lanning.

And he was dead.

11.

The Boss

"Ten feet, then left," I murmured as I crawled along the air duct. I was getting pretty good at this mode of travel. I knew my way around at least half of the underground hallways at the Olde Tyme, via air duct. If I really were planning a heist, I just might be able to pull it off!

I reached the intersection and turned left. Dominic Asher's office was the next vent. I remembered it well—it was the first place I'd climbed into the air ducts this morning. I figured I'd head back there and take another look around the place. As long as I was trapped down here, I might as well make absolutely sure the casino wasn't involved in anything shady.

If only I'd known I was in The Boss's office earlier, I

wouldn't have wasted my time hiding under the desk, I thought. I'd had plenty of time to snoop through the drawers, but I hadn't bothered.

I reached the vent and started to pop the grating out—then stopped. The lights were on. I hadn't left them that way. I pressed my face to the grate and looked down.

There was a man sitting at the desk. Was that The Boss?

He was bald. Well, he had a really lame comb-over of thin brown hair. But from up here, I could see that he was almost entirely bald. And he was typing away at the computer on the desk. I squinted at the screen. It was a spreadsheet of some kind. *Boring.*

I sighed and rested my head on my arms. So much for snooping around Dominic Asher's office. I got the feeling this guy wasn't about to move any-time soon. In fact, he didn't look like the sort of dude to move a lot, ever. *I thought The Boss was supposed to be some kind of hothead. I can't believe the employees are all so afraid of this guy.*

The office door slammed open, making me jump. "Ow!" I yelped as my head bashed against the top of the narrow duct. Lucky for me, the bald guy below was paying more attention to the people walking through his door than to the guy hidden behind the air vent.

"Oh, excuse me, Mr.—" the bald dude started.

But the tall, beefy man in the doorway wasn't about to listen. "What do you think you're doing?" he bellowed. "How dare you just walk right in here? Who told you you could use my computer?"

"Mr. Asher, I am so sorry," the bald guy cried. He frantically tried to gather up the papers he'd scattered around the huge wooden desk.

Ah, so that's *Dominic Asher, The Boss,* I thought as I checked out the big man. He had a thick neck, thick biceps, and what appeared to be a thick skull. *Now I understand why they're scared of him. I wouldn't want to be on his bad side.*

"Doreen, you remember Sam August, don't you?" Asher said, turning to the thin, dark-haired woman behind him. "My accountant?"

"Sure," she replied. "Hi, Sam." She had a Southern accent.

"Uh, hello, Ms. McKenzie," the bald guy replied. He gave up on straightening the desk and just stood there, wringing his hands.

"So what's wrong with your office, Sam?" Asher asked, frowning. "Don't you have a computer there?"

Actually, that is a little weird, I realized. *Why is he in The Boss's office? Especially when The Boss is known to be short-tempered. Everyone else obviously avoids the guy, but Sam the accountant came right in and sat down at his desk. I wonder why.*

SUSPECT PROFILE

Name: Samuel August

Hometown: Hawthorne, NJ

Physical description: Age 48, 5'9", 154 lbs., balding

Occupation: Accountant for the Olde Tyme Resort and Casino

Background: Unknown

Suspicious behavior: Found using Dominic Asher's computer without permission

Suspected of: Rigging slot machines; kidnapping Kathy Boutry.

Possible motive: To prevent Kathy from writing an exposé about the rigged slot machines at the Olde Tyme Casino.

"I'm, um, I was just pulling up the quarterly statement for Ms. McKenzie," Sam stammered. "I got a call from the Office of the Gaming Commission and they said an agent was coming today to do a check."

Asher's frown grew deeper. "I thought this was supposed to be a random check," he said to Doreen.

"It was." Now she was frowning at Sam too.

"Oh . . . whoops," Sam replied. "I guess your assistant didn't know that, Ms. McKenzie. She called to find out if you had arrived yet, so . . ."

"She's new," Doreen said. "I suppose it doesn't matter. I'm here now, so let's go over the Olde Tyme's earnings."

Sam turned the monitor on the desk so that Doreen and Asher could see it. "Everything is in order," he told them. "I've got all of our earnings broken down by category. There's the hotel, the restaurant and the other food concessions—"

"She's from the Gaming Office, Sam," Asher said impatiently. "She doesn't care about the hotel stuff, just the casino."

"Right." Sam ran a nervous hand over his bald head. "Well, the casino payouts are organized by type, as well. There's blackjack, roulette, poker, slot machines—"

"It's mostly the slots I want to see," Doreen told him. "We've heard some rumblings about the payout being low."

"Oh no, not at all," Sam assured her. "Our slot machines pay out eighty-three percent, as required by law."

"I'm sure it's fine. I'll just need to look over the statement," Doreen said with a smile.

Asher nodded. "Of course. Listen, I have a call to make in here. Do you mind if I set you up in the conference room to look at it?" He didn't wait for her to answer. "Sam, print that out, would you?"

As Sam rushed to hit Print, I hurried forward through the air duct. If Dominic Asher was going to make a private call, I wanted to be in on it. And I knew exactly how to do it. On my travels through the air ducts, I'd spotted a private bathroom attached to Asher's office. It was swanky, with its own shower and dressing room—and its own phone.

I slid the grate off the vent and let myself down into the shower. In the office, I heard Doreen and Sam leaving. I waited until I heard Asher's voice booming through the air before I opened the shower door and snuck over to the phone in the dressing room. One light was lit up, so I knew that was the line The Boss was calling from. I studied the phone. A lot of offices use a phone that allows assistants to listen in on their boss's calls so they can take minutes.

Got it, I thought, noticing a button that said MONITOR. I pushed the button, and the light on the line began to blink. I picked up the phone . . . and I was in.

". . . favor to ask, Dad," Dominic Asher's voice was saying. "I have a problem—"

"You always have a problem," a deep, booming voice replied. The Boss's father, I assumed. He did not sound happy. "What is it this time? You need more money? Haven't I already given you enough?"

"It's not—"

"It's not a gift, it's a loan," his father interrupted in a mocking tone. "'I'm going to pay you back, Dad, I promise.' Seems like I've heard that before."

"No. Dad, I don't need money," Dominic said. "If you would just let me talk—"

"Fine. Talk. But don't expect anything from me if you're in trouble with the law again." I could practically see his father crossing his arms over his chest and frowning disapprovingly. I guessed maybe Dominic's dad hadn't been too thrilled when his son was shipped off to prison.

"Okay. I just need a little help with the Gaming Commission," Dominic said. "They're on my back—"

"What did I just say?" his father exploded. "You're in trouble with the law!"

Wow, I thought. *The Boss's father is kind of a jerk. I guess the apple doesn't fall far from the tree.* Although, to be fair, Dominic was actually in trouble with the law. Maybe his father was right to yell at him.

"I am not," The Boss shouted. "You never listen! You never even let me finish a sentence!"

He was met with stony silence. I held my breath, afraid they might hear me breathing.

"Thank you," Dominic went on, his voice cold. "What I was saying is that there's a gaming inspector here right now and she says they've heard rumors about my slot machines."

"And?" his father prompted.

"Well . . . there have been a lot of complaints," Dominic admitted. "For several months now."

"And you're letting the complaints leak out and reach the Gaming Commission?" his father asked. "Are you an idiot?"

Harsh, I thought.

"I don't know how the Gaming Commission found out," Dominic snapped. "I have ways of dealing with the complaints in house, but I can't control whether or not people call the Commission on me."

"Then you'd better fix the slot machines," his father replied.

Sounds like the slot machines are already fixed, I thought. *Fixed to keep anyone from winning.*

"Is that all you have to say?" The Boss asked his dad.

"What did you expect me to say? That I would bribe the Gaming Commissioner for you? We don't all operate the way you do, you know."

"I don't want you to bribe anyone. I just thought you could call the Commissioner and ask him to back off a little bit," Dominic said. "You play golf with him, don't you?"

His father snorted. "You think I'm going to ruin my relationship with a good golfer just to save your butt?"

"It's only asking him for a favor. It won't ruin your relationship." Dominic's voice was growing angry again. I figured it would be pretty upsetting to have your father refuse to help you, even if you were trying to get away with something illegal.

"You know what, son, I will help you," The Boss's father said suddenly.

"You will?"

"Yeah. I'm calling my loan."

There was a long silence. When Dominic spoke again, his voice was brimming with fury. "What loan?"

"The down payment on the Olde Tyme," his father replied. "I want it back. All of it."

"You gave me the whole thing," Dominic protested. "I can't pay you back right now. It would bankrupt me."

"Fine," his dad said. "Then maybe I'll just take over."

"Excuse me?" The Boss's voice was growing louder and louder. "Take over what?"

"The casino. The whole resort. You obviously don't know how to handle the pressure," his father said. "I must have been crazy, putting my money into that place. You have no idea how to run a business. You couldn't even keep yourself out of the slammer."

"That was so long ago—"

"You want me to help you get rid of the Gaming Commissioner?" The Boss's dad cut in. "Then sign the place over to me. Otherwise, you're on your own."

I heard Dominic mutter something under his breath. There was a click, then a dial tone. He had hung up on his father.

A second later, a loud banging sound rang through the air. Followed by another, then another. The painting over the sink rattled with the impact of something heavy on the other side of the wall. I could only guess that The Boss was throwing stuff around in his office. The dude was seriously angry.

I'd better get out of here, I thought. *If he catches me here when he's in a mood like this, he just might kill me.*

As I started for the air vent, it suddenly grew

quiet in the office. I hesitated. Had The Boss left the room? Had he accidentally knocked himself out with his own stapler?

A muffled voice sounded through the air. It was Dominic, talking to someone. I glanced at the phone. The line was lit up again. He was on another call.

I pushed the Monitor button and picked up the phone.

". . . Gaming Commission badgering me all the time," The Boss was saying. "They send people practically every week!"

"But they haven't found anything, have they?" another man's voice replied.

"No. It doesn't matter, though," The Boss said. "It's all going wrong. We've got complaints about the slots, complaints about the plumbing in the hotel, complaints about the food in the restaurant. I'm losing control of it, Billy. I think my father was right."

"Don't say that," Billy answered.

"I mean it," Asher insisted. "He said I wasn't cut out to run things. He said I couldn't handle the pressure."

"He was wrong," Billy said. "Look, you're just upset about all the complaints. It's nothing but a customer service issue. You want me to come over and check it out? Maybe I can help you figure out what to do."

"Yeah." Asher sighed. "That would be great. Maybe I just need to talk it through, figure out what to do with all these people."

"Okay. I'll be there in ten minutes," Billy said. "Meet you in the lobby?"

"Yep. Thanks, man. I've just got to stop the complaints once and for all."

I hit the Monitor button again and hung up the phone. I wasn't sure I liked the way Asher talked about stopping the complaints, but I could worry about that later. For now, I just knew it was time to make a break for it.

The Boss was going upstairs to meet this Billy guy. That meant he would be heading for the elevator and taking it up. If I could figure out how to get into the elevator shaft, I could ride on top of the elevator back up to the casino.

I swung myself back up into the duct and crawled for the hallway. I couldn't climb out a vent into a crowded hall, so I had to find a utility closet or something. I stopped at every vent and peered through to see where it came out. The third vent let out into a room that was completely dark. *That might be a closet,* I thought. I slid down into the room and reached for the doorknob.

". . . getting more and more complaints," a woman's voice said out in the hallway. I froze, my hand on the knob. Somebody was standing right outside. "If you want me to keep ignoring them, you're going to have to give me more money," she went on, her voice lilting with a Southern accent.

That's the Gaming Commission woman, I realized. *Doreen.*

"Don't get greedy," a man's voice replied quietly. "I'll give you the usual amount and no more. Your butt is on the line too."

I let go of the doorknob and leaned against the wall of the dark closet. My mind was racing. Someone was giving Doreen money to ignore complaints?

He's bribing her, I realized. *Kathy was right. The Boss is bribing the gaming inspector. The slot machines really are rigged!*

SUSPECT PROFILE

Name: Doreen McKenzie

Hometown: Jersey City, NJ

Physical description: Age 33, 5'4", 110 lbs., shoulder-length dark hair

Occupation: Gaming inspector

Background: Moved to New Jersey from Georgia; has worked at the Gaming Commission for two years

<u>Suspicious behavior:</u> Overheard taking bribe

<u>Suspected of:</u> Colluding with the Olde Tyme
in rigging their slot machines

<u>Possible motive:</u> Greed

FRANK

12.
Upping the Ante

"It's a good thing you called us, son," the lead detective told me. "I'd say this poor guy has been lying here for at least two days. Who knows when he would've been found if you hadn't come along."

"Yeah," I said. "I guess that's what happens when you live alone, huh? Nobody knows whether you're okay or not."

"Mmm." The detective chewed on her lip, studying me. "What did you say you were doing here again?"

"Working on a newspaper story," I said. I was starting to get used to that cover story. "On gambling. Milton had made complaints against the Olde Tyme Casino, and I've been talking to all the complainants."

"Oh, yeah? What did he complain about?" the detective asked, pulling out her notebook.

"I'm not really sure," I said truthfully. "It's not my story, I'm just doing the grunt work."

She nodded, taking notes. "What paper?"

"Um, the *Press of Atlantic City*," I said. "If it even gets published. My boss is a freelancer, so she works for a lot of papers."

The detective looked me up and down, then nodded. "That's very helpful, thanks."

"No problem," I said, relieved. Clearly she had decided I was telling the truth. "What do you think killed him?" I asked, shooting another look at Milton Lanning. I hadn't gotten too close to the body before I called the cops.

"Blunt force, I'd say," the detective replied. "I've got men searching the premises for a murder weapon. Probably a shovel, a hammer, something like that. Maybe even an iron skillet."

I shook my head. "I can't believe somebody killed him," I said grimly. This was getting serious. Obviously somebody had wanted to shut Milton up about the slots, and the same person probably paid Edna a visit too. That's why she was so scared when I mentioned the Olde Tyme.

And what if that guy has Kathy? What if he has Joe?

"Do you mind if I take off now?" I asked the detective.

"Go ahead, we've already got your statement," she replied. "We'll call if we have any other questions."

I gave her a wave and headed for my motorcycle. I had to get to the casino—immediately. I hit the gas and took the bike as fast as it would go. Every so often Joe and I broke the speed laws when we were on a case. If a cop stopped us, we could show them our ATAC badges. But that had never happened—our bikes are so fast that I doubt anyone could catch up!

At the Olde Tyme, I parked my motorcycle next to Joe's and sprinted for the stairs. My brother was missing and he might be in danger. I wasn't in the mood to be polite. I ran right up to the concierge desk and got in the guy's face. "I want to know who's in charge of answering customer complaints," I demanded.

The concierge blinked in surprise. "Do you have a complaint?"

"No. I'm the assistant to Kathy Boutry, a reporter who's doing a story on your rigged slot machines," I replied. "I know how many people have complained about the slots. Now I want to know who those complaints go to. Who's the one dealing with it?"

"What's that supposed to mean, 'dealing with it'?" a man bellowed from inside the office behind the concierge desk. "Who's asking about the slots?" A big guy came striding out. His neck was so thick that I was surprised his tie fit around it. His face was bright red.

"I am," I told him. "I want to know—"

"I heard what you want," he snapped. "Here's what I want. I want you to keep your nose out of my casino's business."

"Your casino?" I asked. "Who are you?"

"Dominic Asher. This is my place, and I want you out!"

"I asked a simple question," I argued.

Asher got so close to me that I thought he was going to try to bump chests like a baseball player arguing with an umpire. "I've had enough of you people—" he began.

"Hey, hey, calm down," another guy cried, rushing over and grabbing Asher by the arm. "You don't want to talk to a customer that way."

"He's a reporter, Billy, not a customer," Asher snapped. But he let the guy pull him away.

"Sorry about that," Billy said to me over his shoulder. "Dom's under a lot of pressure lately. If you want to make an appointment, I'm sure he'll be happy to talk to you." He led Dominic back into the office and shut the door behind them.

I glanced at the concierge. He shrugged apologetically. "People do win at slots, you know," he told me. "Mr. Asher has a bad temper, but he's not cheating anyone."

"Can you prove that?" I asked.

"Sure." The concierge handed me a sheet of paper with a bunch of small photographs of grinning people. Along the top, in old-fashioned–looking calligraphy, was written "I had a grand Olde Tyme and won big!"

It was pretty cheesy.

"What's this?" I asked.

"That's our list of slot machine winners," he told me cheerfully. "See? There's a lot of them!"

Yeah, too many, I thought. It seemed pretty convenient that the Olde Tyme had a preprinted list of winners to hand out. The complaints about the slots were obviously getting to them. "So I guess people ask about the slots a lot, huh? Why else would you have this all ready to go?"

The guy's smile faltered. "Well . . . yes. A few customers have suggested that the machines have been tampered with. Our accountant told me to give this list to anyone who asks."

"You have phone numbers for any of these people?" I asked.

The concierge looked appalled. "I can't give out their numbers. That's private."

Doesn't matter. I'll get their numbers myself, I thought

as I turned away. I went up to our room, hoping against hope that Joe was there.

No such luck. His stuff was still thrown all over the place, but he was gone.

I pushed down my worry and focused on trying to figure out what was happening at the casino. Worrying wasn't going to help Joe. Solving the case was. I pulled out my cell and dialed Vijay.

"Patel," he answered. "Did you find Joe yet, Frank?"

"Not yet," I told him. "I need you to look up some names for me. I just need phone numbers."

"Go ahead."

I glanced at the name of the first winner. "Jan Mistel." While Vijay did his magic, I studied the sheet of winners. There were photographs, but they weren't labeled. I had no idea which one of these smiling people was Jan Mistel. Something about this so-called winners' list didn't sit right with me.

"Can't find her," Vijay said.

"Huh?"

"I can't find her," he repeated. "No address, no phone, nothing."

"Where are you looking?" I asked.

"All the usual places. People finders, white pages, that kind of stuff," Vijay said.

"Maybe she's unlisted," I said. "Try Brian Guer-ther."

Vijay was quiet for a minute. Then he said, "Same thing."

"Sueann Perasol?"

But he couldn't find her, either.

"What's going on?" I asked him. "They can't all be unlisted. Do you think the hotel just made them up?"

"You mean they just came up with names and slapped them on a piece of paper?" Vijay asked doubtfully. "That would be kind of stupid, wouldn't it? If a reporter like Kathy wanted to do fact-checking, she could find out right away that these were made-up names."

"Well, we can't find the people," I pointed out. "The Olde Tyme wants everyone to think that people win at their slot machines. So they say all these people have won. How would anyone know if it was a lie? We can't even prove that these people exist."

"Sure, we can," Vijay said. "I can check their Social Security records."

"Really?" I asked.

"Yeah. With ATAC's access, I can check tax records, too. Or I can check birth and death records. Or . . ." Vijay stopped talking for a second as he realized what he was saying. "Um . . . do you want me to do that?" he asked. "I guess you could've checked the white pages yourself."

"I guess," I said, smiling. "Although I don't really need to know their Social Security numbers. What I need to know is if they really won money at the Olde Tyme's slot machines."

"You know, I'm not finding any of them in the IRS database either," Vijay said slowly. "That's really weird. Everybody has to pay taxes. And people who won money would have a lot of taxes to pay. . . ."

"Try birth certificates," I suggested.

There was a long silence. Then Vijay gave a low whistle. "I found Jan," he said.

"Great. Where is she?"

"In the Blessed Souls Cemetery in Brooklyn," Vijay replied. "She's been dead for thirty years."

What? I thought. "What?" I said.

"Brian is there too. And Sueann," Vijay went on. "They all died as children. That's why there are no tax records. They never grew up and had jobs."

"So the casino didn't make these people up," I said.

"No," Vijay replied. "They're all real people. They're real people who died years before the Olde Tyme Casino opened for business."

"Which means they're real people who absolutely did not win at the slot machines," I said. "That clinches it. The Olde Tyme Casino is perpetrating a fraud. They're criminals."

"And they have Joe," Vijay said.

13.
Proof

"Hello, old friend," I said to the grate over the vent in Dominic Asher's office. "I'm back again." I pulled the grate off and dropped it down onto The Boss's desk with a clatter. I didn't mind the noise—I knew Asher wasn't there. He was busy meeting his friend Billy upstairs in the lobby.

Which meant I had time to check out his computer for myself.

I lowered myself down to the desk, then plopped into the cushy leather chair. Sam the accountant had left the files open when The Boss shooed him out of the office. All I had to do was hit the space bar to wake up the computer.

The spreadsheet popped up, listing all kinds of earnings from the various parts of the Olde Tyme

Resort and Casino. What a yawn. Still, if I wanted to prove that there was something illegal going on here, I might need this stuff. I sent the file to the printer.

If Asher is bribing the Gaming Commission to overlook the complaints about his slot machines, that means the slot machines are rigged, I thought. But this quarterly report showed the slots giving the legally required payout.

"Where's the real info?" I asked the computer. "He's got to keep track of his actual earnings somehow."

I minimized the spreadsheet and took a look at the other files on the computer. Most of them had a little symbol that indicated they were locked. But there were two folders still open from when Sam had been on the computer. I clicked on the first one.

It was labeled "Dailies."

Inside was a slew of files with names like poker2tuesday and roulette6friday.

I clicked on blackjack1monday. The file wasn't very big. It was just a list of numbers, but the header on top cleared things up for me. It listed the dealers who had worked Blackjack Table Number One on Monday. Underneath each dealer's name was a running total of bets placed, money won by the customers, and money won by the house.

"Interesting," I murmured. "Let's see what the dailies show for the slot machines."

I opened slot24tuesday and gazed at a long list of statistics. There was no way I could understand what this file was telling me, not without studying it for a lot longer. I didn't have the time. But that didn't mean I couldn't use the information to bring down Dominic Asher and the Olde Tyme Casino.

I selected about twenty different files from various slot machines and sent them to the printer.

The machine came to life with a loud whirring noise. The pages of the quarterly report began spitting out of it . . . slowly. I rolled my eyes. They had a vault full of cash at this place, but their printer was just as slow as mine.

Clearly, I had some time to kill before all my files were done printing. I looked around and reached for the phone. Could I call Frank from here? Would anyone notice the phone line lighting up?

I hesitated.

My brother would be able to help me get out of this basement maze of offices. And he was probably pretty worried about me by now.

But the security guards were still looking for me. Chances were good that they'd notice anything out of the ordinary. They would know Asher wasn't in his office—their monitors would show him upstairs. So if his phone lines lit up, they'd come to check it out.

I couldn't risk it.

"Well, at least I can search the desk," I muttered, pulling open the top drawer. Inside was a stapler and a package full of tiny Post-it note pads. The second drawer had a pile of brochures for the Olde Tyme. The bottom drawer had a box of paper clips and a photo of Dominic Asher and some guy who looked like an older version of him. Probably his father, I figured. Although I didn't know why he would keep a family photo in his bottom drawer.

"So much for the incriminating evidence hidden in his desk," I said aloud. I glanced at the printer. It had just finished printing the first spreadsheet. I still had a long wait ahead of me.

Bored, I spun the leather chair around. The suit jacket over the back of it swung out as I turned, the sleeves rising into the air as if there were ghostly arms inside. I put my feet down to stop spinning and pulled the jacket toward me.

As I checked the pockets for anything unusual, I took another look at the printer. A few of the slot machine daily reports had come out. I stuck my hand into the inside pocket and found a key card for the hotel. Room 602.

That's weird, I thought. *Why does Asher have a room key? Does he live here?*

"I'm telling you, I heard something," a voice said suddenly.

My heart gave a loud thump. The voice was right outside the door.

"We're not supposed to go into The Boss's office," another voice argued.

I shot a look at the printer. The daily reports were still coming. I couldn't wait for it to finish.

I raced over and grabbed the stack of papers that had already printed. Then I shoved them into the back pocket of my jeans, stuck the hotel key in my shirt pocket, and jumped up to grab the vent.

Too late.

The door opened, and Gigantor stepped inside. "Freeze!" he yelled, pointing a gun at me.

I was caught!

14.
A Lucky Break

"Okay, what do I know?" I said out loud. I was at that point in the case where I had lots of info, but no real answers.

Whenever we're in that situation, Joe always says we should do a recap. He likes to list everything we know, then everyone we suspect, and then see if we've got a solid lead. And it usually works.

"I know that the Olde Tyme is lying about the slot machine winners. They've put together a page full of names, but none of the people listed have ever really won. None of them are even still alive."

I paced up and down near the foot of my hotel bed.

"So that means the casino is actively trying to cover up . . . something. Probably the fact that the slot machines are fixed so that they don't pay out to the customers. The casino keeps all the money from the slots."

What else? Joe's voice asked in my head.

"I know that one person who registered a complaint about the slot machines is dead. And that another person is terrified. And that means that somebody is willing to use violence to keep the truth from coming out."

I stopped walking as the truth hit me. Edna was scared. Milton was dead. Both of them had made complaints to the Olde Tyme. They had more than gambling in common. They also had a visitor in common. The guy who had killed Milton was probably the same one who had scared Edna. Which meant that she knew who he was. Even if he was just some kind of enforcer and not the mastermind behind whatever was going on here, he was a step in the right direction. If I found that guy, maybe I could find Kathy.

Maybe I could find my brother.

I had to convince Edna to talk to me. I knew she was scared, but now that I'd discovered the Olde Tyme was willing to commit murder, it was more important than ever to speak to Edna. There was a killer on the loose!

I grabbed my cell phone and got the number for the

Sunny Tomorrows Senior Living retirement home.

"Sunny Tomorrows," a cheerful voice on the other end of the line answered.

"Hi. Is Edna Williams available?" I asked.

"Who's calling?"

"Um . . ." What could I say? Who would Edna talk to? Definitely not anybody from the Olde Tyme Casino—just the name had been enough to seriously freak out the poor old woman. But if Edna came to this place a lot, maybe she went to other casinos as well. It was worth a shot. "This is Frank H-Harding," I fumbled, suddenly remembering that I had left her my name. "I'm calling from the Atlantic City Board of Tourism with a special offer for Edna Williams."

"A special offer?" The receptionist sounded skeptical.

"Yes. She's won a weekend stay at one of our hotel casinos," I said. I tried to sound like one of those salespeople on a TV commercial.

"Hold on, I'll see if she wants to talk to you," the receptionist said. A second later some lame Muzak came on the line. The next thing I heard was Edna's voice.

"Hello?" she asked. She was back to sounding spry and cheerful, and I felt a little bad. I was kind of ambushing the old lady. *If I can get this case solved, she will be safer,* I told myself.

"Hello, Mrs. Williams," I said. "This is Frank H—"

"Hardy. Yes, I know," she cut in.

"You do?" I asked, surprised.

"Of course I do," she replied. "My hair may be gray, but the brain underneath it is still sharp, Frank. If you were really from some tourism board, I wouldn't have taken your call."

"Oh," I said. I was confused. "I thought if I said who I really was, you *definitely* wouldn't have talked to me."

"Yes, I can see why you think that. I'm sorry I slammed the door on you," Edna said. "I was afraid and I acted like a silly little bird."

"I understand," I told her. "But I want to help you. That's why—"

"You want to help me, and I want to help you," Edna said. "I'm ashamed of myself. I acted like a coward when I kicked you out. Can you come back and see me?"

"Will the security guards let me?" I asked.

Edna chuckled. "I'll let them know it's okay," she promised. "Although they'll probably stick around to make sure you're on the up-and-up, Frank."

"Sure," I said.

"I promise I won't close the door on you this time," she said. "I'll see you soon."

When I got to the retirement home, Edna was

waiting in the garden. One of the security guards who'd escorted me out stood nearby.

"I've thought it through and I decided I can trust you," the old lady said when she saw me. "You're not like that other one."

"What other one?" I asked, sitting down next to her on the wooden bench.

"There was a fellow here last week, a nasty fellow," Edna told me with a shudder. "He came right into my room without even knocking. He said . . . he said he'd kill me if I ever went near the Olde Tyme Casino again."

A chill ran down my spine at the thought of this sweet old lady being threatened like that. But I knew it wasn't an empty threat. Somebody had murdered Milton Lanning. Chances were that they'd kill Edna Williams, too, if she didn't do as she was told. I tried not to think about the fact that Joe could be at that same person's mercy that very moment.

"Do you go to the Olde Tyme a lot?" I asked her.

"There's a group of us who go every Tuesday," Edna replied. "A bus comes to the retirement home, and anybody who's feeling up to it goes for the afternoon. It's something to do, you understand? Ah, you're too young to understand." Her eyes twinkled. "You see, Frank, when you get to be an old person like me, you'll realize that things can be pretty boring sometimes."

"I already realize that," I assured her.

"It's nice to get away from the retirement home," Edna said. "The restaurant at the Olde Tyme serves a nice chocolate malted, and the theme of the whole place is old-fashioned. We all like it there."

"Okay," I said. "So why did somebody threaten you?"

"Well, old folks don't have a lot of money to waste," Edna told me. "So we don't go playing card games for money. We mostly stick to the slot machines. They're fun, and they're set up to let you get a bang for your buck."

I grinned.

"You can sit for hours at a slot machine," Edna went on. "You give it your nickels or your pennies, and every so often it gives them back. Just a little here and there, to keep you playing for a while longer."

"But the machines at the Olde Tyme don't ever pay out any money," I guessed.

Edna nodded. "That's right. They're old-fashioned slot machines, and everybody loves them. But none of us ever hit a jackpot. That's not normal, Frank. And I know what I'm talking about. I've been to my share of casinos. We all have." She gave me a wink.

"Old folks and slot machines go together like peanut butter and jelly."

"So you complained to the management," I said.

"That I did," Edna confirmed. "We all knew something was wrong with those machines. I'm the only one who had the guts to say anything about it. Now I wish I hadn't." Her face fell as she thought about it. "Bad enough they try to cheat us old folks out of our money. But to send a thug to threaten me? It's terrible."

"I couldn't agree more," I said. "What did this man look like? I need to find him. You're . . . you're not the only one he's visited."

Edna pursed her lips and gazed at me. "Are you telling me he did worse than threaten someone?"

"Yes," I admitted. "I'm afraid that another person who filed a complaint with the Olde Tyme is dead."

Edna's eyes widened.

"I don't mean to scare you," I said. "I just think you should keep your friend there close by for a while." I nodded toward the security guard.

"I will," Edna promised.

"So the man who threatened you," I said, "can you describe him?"

The old woman frowned. "Well, I'll try. Let's see. He was older than you. Not much to look at, to tell the truth. Brown hair, brown eyes, I think. I was too frightened to pay attention to his appearance. I'm sorry."

"That's all right," I assured her. But I couldn't help feeling a bit disappointed. I had come all the way back here, and Edna didn't have anything useful to tell me. "Thank you for letting me know about this."

I stood up to go, but Edna put her hand on my arm. "Wait. I wanted to give you something. Your friend Kathy Boutry left this with me," she said. "She was asking if I'd ever seen this gentleman at the casino, but I haven't." She handed me a photograph.

Of Saul Gold, the CEO of MetaChem.

"Kathy Boutry gave you this?" I asked.

Edna nodded. "Does that help you?"

"I don't know," I said truthfully. "I know who this man is, but I have no idea what his connection to the Olde Tyme casino is."

I frowned at the picture. MetaChem . . . and the casino. Those were two different articles, weren't they?

But apparently Kathy thought there was some connection.

And I had to find out what it was.

JOE

15.
Caught!

"Get him!" Gigantor yelled.

I frantically tried to pull my weight up into the air duct, but it was too late. The huge dude ran across the room and grabbed my ankle. Holding on with my fingertips, I swung myself around and kicked him—hard—with my free foot.

"Oof!" Gigantor fell back, his fingers slipping off of me.

I jerked my legs up, going for the relative safety of the duct.

But three other guards had spilled into the office behind Gigantor. One of them pushed past him and jumped up onto the desk, reaching for me.

I pulled back both my legs and aimed a kick at

him. My sneakers hit him square in the chest and he stumbled backward, falling off the desk.

One more time, I tried to pull myself up into the duct. But by this time my arms were aching from the effort of holding on for so long. When Gigantor grabbed me again, I fell.

I snagged him in a headlock on the way, taking him down with me. I landed on top of him and jabbed my elbow into his ribs to knock the wind out of him. He gasped, out of commission.

Jumping to my feet, I turned to face the other three.

It didn't look good. All of them stood between me and the door.

The first one took a swing at me. I ducked under his arm and chopped him in the back, in between his shoulder blades. He stumbled forward, and I used his own momentum against him, shoving him into Gigantor on the ground.

The next guard moved forward and aimed a punch at my stomach. That one was too low to duck. I spun away, but he managed to get me in the side. I grabbed his other arm, dug my shoulder into him, and flipped him over my back. He crashed into the first guard, who was just getting up.

Now there was only one guy left between me

and the door. I ran for it. But the third guard finally got smart. He didn't try to hit me. He just launched himself at me, wrapped his arms around my legs, and tackled me to the ground.

Before I could even get a punch in, the second guard threw himself over my chest. The first one slapped a pair of cuffs onto my wrists.

They had me.

"Get him up," Gigantor wheezed. "Put him in the chair."

The other three pulled me off the ground and shoved me into the big leather desk chair. Gigantor pulled out his walkie-talkie. "Tell The Boss we caught the intruder," he said. "In his office."

"On my way," Asher's voice came back through the crackle of static.

The guards exchanged nervous glances. All four of them looked at me. Gigantor shook his head. "Geez, he's just a kid," he muttered.

I didn't say anything. But I was a little nervous too. Dominic Asher had anger management issues, everybody knew it. And now I was going to have to face him with my hands cuffed. It didn't look good.

Two minutes later, The Boss appeared in the doorway.

Asher looked me up and down, then turned to

Gigantor. "This is the thief you've been looking for all morning?"

"I'm not a thief," I piped up.

Asher laughed. "I can see *that*."

"He's been in the air ducts. That's why we didn't find him," Gigantor said. "He was going for the duct when we caught him."

The Boss glanced up at the open vent over his desk. "Smart," he commented. "What are you doing here, kid? The casino offices are a restricted area, as I'm sure you knew."

"It was a bet," I blurted out. "My brother and I are staying in the hotel and we saw the signs for the service elevator. You know, that it's restricted, like you said." I paused and drew in a breath, stalling while I tried to figure out what to say. "So, uh, he bet me that I couldn't get into the secure area. And I said I could. And he said no way and bet me fifty bucks. So I had to do it."

The Boss just raised his eyebrows.

"So I got down here and I won the bet," I babbled on. "But then when I tried to get back out to collect my fifty, all the doors were locked and I was trapped down here."

"That's true, sir, we went into lockdown when we found out there was an intruder," Gigantor said.

I kept my mouth shut. There was nothing else I could say. Either The Boss believed me or he didn't. His face was impossible to read.

"A fifty-dollar bet?" he finally asked.

I nodded.

The Boss laughed. "That's a lot of money." He turned to Gigantor. "Uncuff him, give him back his phone."

Gigantor looked relieved, but it couldn't compare with how I felt. Asher had bought my story!

"You won your bet," The Boss told me. "But thanks to this little stunt, you're not welcome at the Olde Tyme anymore. Get your brother and get out of here."

I gaped at him. That was it? That was all he was going to do to me? I thought about the key card I'd taken from the jacket on the back of his chair—the key to room 602. What was in that room?

"Um . . . can I get my stuff first?" I asked. "From my room?"

Asher waved his hand at Gigantor. "Take him to his room first, then make sure he leaves."

The first guard unlocked the cuffs from my wrists, and Gigantor pulled me to my feet. "Let's go," he said. The Boss didn't even glance in my direction as I followed Gigantor from the room. We got into the service elevator. "What's your room number?" he asked.

"6-0-2," I lied.

He didn't say anything as we rode up to the sixth floor, and neither did I. I was still trying to figure out what the deal was with Dominic Asher. Why had he just let me go?

The elevator reached the sixth floor, and the doors opened. I confidently led the way to room 602, Gigantor on my heels. The key card I had taken from Asher's office was in my jeans pocket. I pulled it out and stuck it into the door of room 602.

"I'll only be a few minutes," I told Gigantor.

Then I pushed open the door to the room, wondering what I'd find.

It was dark inside. But I could still see Kathy Boutry on the couch in the sitting area, her hands and feet tied.

Her eyes went wide with surprise when she saw me. "Who are *you*?" she asked.

"I'm Joe Hardy. I've been looking for you," I said, rushing over to her. She was tied up with some kind of thin rope, like a clothesline. I quickly loosened the knots around her hands, and Kathy bent to untie her feet.

"We gotta get out of here before The Boss realizes that I found you," I told her, heading for the door.

Between the two of us, Kathy and I should be able to take out Gigantor. Then we would run for the stairs, get down to the garage, and escape on my bike before Dominic Asher knew what had happened.

Kathy pulled the ropes off her feet. I reached for the door handle—just as the door swung open.

Sam August, the accountant, stepped inside.

And pointed a gun at me.

16.
Haz-Mat

Lucy Lopez smiled up at me from behind her desk at MetaChem. "Hey there!" she chirped. "What brings you back here?"

I forced myself to meet her eyes and put on a smile. I needed her help. Somehow there was a connection between Kathy's MetaChem story and the Olde Tyme Casino. I had to figure it out, and fast. Lucy was my best chance to do that.

I had to get her to like me, which meant I had to flirt with her. It's what Joe would do. *She's a cute, nice girl,* I told myself. *Don't be such a wuss.*

"Honestly, I was hoping you could help me out, Lou," I told her. "You seem like somebody who knows things."

"I know you like me," she replied.

"See?" I forced myself to ignore the blush that was creeping up my cheeks.

Lucy giggled.

"Here's the thing," I said. "You remember that reporter I work for, Kathy Boutry? Well, she's gonna be really mad if I don't finish fact-checking this story. That's why I wanted to talk to Sollie."

"Sollie hates reporters," Lou said. "But I don't."

"Great. Well, Kathy's writing an article about some illegal dumping that MetaChem has been doing—dumping toxic waste and infecting the reservoir. Do you know anything about that? I won't tell anyone I heard it from you."

Lucy rolled her eyes. "Oh, please. We don't dump anything into the water. All our hazardous materials are handled by a company that specializes in that kind of thing. MetaChem would never pollute the environment. Your friend Kathy got it wrong."

"So there's a whole outside company that handles the dumping?" I asked.

"Mm-hmm. BB's Waste Management. They come every morning and take our toxins for disposal. I can give you the address if you want."

"Yeah," I said eagerly. As she wrote it on a slip of paper, I glanced around. The door to Sollie's office was closed. I leaned closer to Lucy. "Hey, listen, about Sollie . . . I heard he likes to gamble."

She frowned. "Not that I know of."

"Are you sure?" I asked. "Doesn't he hang out at the Olde Tyme Casino?"

Lou snorted. "No. Way. Are you kidding? He hates that place. If anybody even mentions it, he gets all mean and yells. And he's pretty scary when he yells."

Well, at least now I know that Sollie has some kind of issue with the Olde Tyme, I thought. "Why does he hate it so much?"

"How should I know?" Lucy asked. "He won't talk about it." She held the waste company's address out to me, but when I reached for it, she snatched her hand back. "First you have to promise to take me out to dinner this weekend," she said playfully.

There was no way to fight the blush now. "Sure," I said awkwardly.

"Good." She handed me the paper. "I put my number on there too."

"Okay. Thanks." I fled.

The waste management company was located a mile down the road from MetaChem. When I pulled into the parking lot, I had to double-check the address. It was just a small, rundown brick building without so much as a sign out front. But the address matched the one Lucy had given me.

As I started to get off the motorcycle, a truck pulled around from the back of the building. It was a medium-size white truck with a hand-painted sign on the side that read BB'S WASTE MANAGEMENT.

I bent over, pretending to fiddle with something on my bike as the truck pulled past me and turned out onto the road. Then I gunned the engine and followed it.

I was getting to know this area pretty well with all the driving around I had done today. The truck was heading for the heavily wooded area near where Milton Lanning's trailer was. Without warning, it suddenly hung a left onto a tiny, winding lane that led into the trees.

I stopped my bike and checked it out. A chain-link fence ran along the tree line, with a small wooden sign on the post that told me the woods were part of Hammonton Lake State Park. I watched the taillights of the truck disappear into the forest. Should I follow it? I couldn't help thinking this was a waste of time.

What did it have to do with the slot machines at the Olde Tyme Casino? I still didn't know how Sollie was linked to the place. And I was worried about Joe and Kathy.

Kathy was investigating MetaChem too, I reminded myself. *Just because the Olde Tyme is involved in some crooked stuff doesn't mean that they're the ones who kid-napped Kathy.*

I sighed. I was concerned for my brother. But my mission was to find Kathy Boutry, and I wasn't sure she could take care of herself the way I hoped Joe could. Kathy had been asking people like Edna about Saul Gold. Saul Gold was involved with this other company. So it was possible that the illegal dumping story had led Kathy to BB's Waste Management. I had to stay on the truck.

I turned onto the lane and sped up until I could see the white truck ahead of me. Then I pulled off the pavement. We were in the middle of nowhere. The truck driver would definitely notice a motor-cycle following him.

I kept off-road, veering around trees and bouncing through ditches and small streams, always making sure the white truck was in sight through the forest. Where was this guy going? It wasn't very likely that there was a toxic waste dump out here in the park. I had a bad feeling that Kathy's illegal dumping story was absolutely true.

The truck stopped, right in the middle of the road. *Why not?* I thought. *There's nobody around for miles. Who's going to see?*

I stopped my bike and cut the engine so the driver wouldn't hear it. Then I got off and crept a little closer, crouching in the underbrush to keep out of sight. I pulled out my cell phone and set it up to take pictures. I had a feeling I would want photographic evidence of this.

The driver got out of the truck, pulled on a thick pair of gloves, and opened the back door. He climbed inside and rolled a large metal drum to the edge of the truck bed. I snapped a few photos as he gave it a push that sent the drum flying from the truck. It landed with a thud on the pavement and rolled over until I could see the biohazard sign on the side of it. The driver jumped down and rolled the drum off the side of the road and through the woods for about ten feet—straight toward me. I hit the dirt as he passed. He was only a few feet away, but he didn't see me, and I didn't move.

I heard a splashing sound. Then the driver tromped back through the woods and climbed into the front of the truck. I heard the door slam shut, the engine rev, and the truck drive off. That's when I got up and walked through the woods to the small stream nearby. It was a narrow tributary, but the water was deep and the current was fast. I spotted the biohazard drum about twenty feet away, half hidden by a tangle of tree roots.

I had a feeling I knew where this water was flowing: toward the Hammonton Lake reservoir. So MetaChem's waste was going to end up in the drinking water after all.

But that wasn't the part that surprised me the most.

What surprised me the most was that I had seen the truck driver before. He was Dominic Asher's friend from the Olde Tyme. Billy.

SUSPECT PROFILE

<u>Name:</u> William "Billy" Barton

<u>Hometown:</u> Atlantic City, NJ

<u>Physical desription:</u> Age 38, 5'10", wiry build

<u>Occupation:</u> Owner and sole employee of BB's Waste Management

<u>Background:</u> Did 5 years in prison for extortion

<u>Suspicious behavior:</u> Seen dumping hazardous waste into the public water supply

<u>Suspected of:</u> Illegal dumping

<u>Possible motive:</u> Greed. It doesn't cost anything to dump illegally. He can keep all his company's earnings for himself.

17.
Full House

"How far away are you?" Sam was saying. "Just get here!" He had been on the phone nonstop ever since he'd finished tying my hands together. His back was to me, and he seemed totally engrossed in his conversation.

I leaned toward Kathy, who was tied up next to me on the couch. "What is the accountant doing here?" I whispered.

She stared at me as if I were crazy. "Who?"

"Sam. The accountant." I nodded toward him.

"Why wouldn't he be here?" Kathy whispered back. "He's the one who's been holding me hostage."

"Sam?" I said, surprised. "What about The Boss?"

Kathy shrugged, her eyebrows drawn together in confusion.

"Isn't Dominic Asher the one behind the slot machine scam?" I asked.

"I don't know," Kathy replied. "The only thing I know for sure is that the slot machines here were tampered with to change the probability of winning—it's an old mechanical trick that works with these old-fashioned slots. The newer machines in the big casinos are all computerized now."

"Right," I said. "I met a few ladies who told me that."

"Well, Sam is one of the old-timers who knows how to do it. He served three years in prison for stealing from an Indian casino in California a while back," Kathy told me. "He might know how to cook the books, but he's no accountant."

"So Asher must have hired him to rig the slot machines here," I guessed.

"Maybe," Kathy replied. "He does have a partner—that's who he's talking to now. He's always calling the guy and getting hysterical. I get the feeling Sam is in over his head."

I glanced over at him. He was sweating, and his face looked pale. I couldn't hear what he was saying into the phone, but he certainly didn't look happy.

"The Gaming Commission knows that the slot machines are fixed," I told Kathy. "I overheard Asher bribing the inspector to keep quiet."

"No talking!" Sam snapped, hanging up the phone. He mopped his sweaty brow. "My partner is on the way over. He'll know what to do with the two of you. Until then, just keep quiet." He waved the gun in our direction, but he didn't look dangerous. He looked scared.

I wonder if he even knows how to use that thing, I thought.

"Is that security guard still outside the door?" I asked Sam. "Is he in on this too?"

"No," Sam snapped. "I got rid of him. Now mind your own business. No talking until my partner gets here."

"Isn't Dominic your partner?" I asked. "No wonder you're afraid of him. I heard he's an ex-con. He seems like an angry guy."

Sam stared at me for a moment. Then he laughed. "Dominic? The Boss? Yeah. He was convicted of road rage. He stopped traffic for two hours and some bigwig missed his daughter's wedding, so Dominic went to jail for a few months."

"Wait," I said. "Are you telling me that The Boss isn't the one who—"

"I said shut up!" Sam yelled. "You keep talking.

Don't you know how much trouble you're in? Both of you?"

"I don't think they do," said a voice from the doorway.

I whipped my head toward the newcomer. The dude was thin, but I could see that he was strong. His dark eyes were cold as he gazed at me.

"Billy," Kathy cried. "I should have known!"

"Billy?" I said. "Dominic Asher's friend Billy?"

Sam spun around and pointed the gun at me, his eyes wild. "Right," I said quickly. "I'm shutting up."

Billy chuckled. "You look a little tense, Sam," he said.

"Don't try to be funny," Sam snapped, waving the gun. "I've had it with you. I want out."

Lightning-fast, Billy's hand shot out and snatched the gun away. "Watch where you're pointing that," he said. "And calm down."

"No!" Sam yelled. "I'm done with this. I was fine with rigging the slot machines. I was fine with falsifying the books so Dominic wouldn't notice. But I didn't sign on for kidnapping and murder!"

My throat went dry. *Murder?*

"But you're so good at kidnapping," Billy mocked him. "You're the one who's been holding the girl reporter hostage."

"You told me to!" Sam yelled.

"And like you said, *you're* the one who rigged the slot machines and falsified the financial records. It's all on you, Sam. If you want out, it's fine with me. You're the one who'll be doing time for fraud and embezzling and kidnapping."

Sam's mouth kept opening and closing as if he were a giant goldfish. But Billy looked perfectly relaxed. He was a lot more dangerous than Sam, I could tell. Sam might have done all that stuff, but it was obvious that Billy was the one in charge here.

"N-No," Sam finally sputtered. "You can't stick the whole thing on me. These two are witnesses. They know you're involved now."

Billy glanced at me and Kathy, his eyes like ice. "They won't count as witnesses if they're dead."

I heard Kathy suck in a breath, and she began to squirm around, trying to get her hands free. I was already working on mine, too. I had no doubt that Billy would shoot us if he had to. The guy was cold-blooded.

"You can't keep killing everyone who finds out," Sam snapped.

"Oh, I'm not going to kill these two," Billy said. "You are."

Sam gasped. "I am not. I'm no murderer."

"Fine. I'll take care of the kid." Billy shot me a lazy smile. "But you have to shoot the girl."

"No," Sam said.

Kathy stared at him, terrified.

"Yes. It's the only way, Sam." Billy put his hand on Sam's shoulder. "See, right now you don't sound very loyal to me. You want out, and you want me to take the fall. But I'm not going to do that."

"I won't tell anyone about you," Sam whined. "I swear. I'll just take off. I'll never tell a single person."

"There's only one way I can be sure of that," Billy said in a reasonable voice. "If you kill the girl, then I'll know for sure that you won't talk."

Sam stared, speechless. Billy held out the gun. Slowly, Sam reached for it. He stared down at the weapon in his hand. Then he turned to Kathy. He pointed the gun at her.

"Don't worry, Sammy, we won't get caught," Billy added. "Once they're dead, I'll get rid of the bodies."

"By dumping them in the water with your toxic waste?" asked a new voice.

Frank's voice.

18.

Reunited

"Frank!" my brother called. "What took you so long?"

I shook my head. Leave it to Joe to act like a wise guy while he was tied up and being threatened with death.

I ran straight for the gun. As long as it was pointing at Kathy, nothing else mattered.

The bald guy wasn't holding the pistol very tightly. I jumped up and kicked—right at his forearm. His arm shot back, and the gun went flying. Billy tackled me from behind, his arms catching me around the waist and dragging me to the floor.

It was a pretty good takedown, but the guy wasn't very big. I outweighed him by at least twenty pounds. I scrambled onto my back and shoved him in the chest.

"Oof!" The air left his lungs as he fell off me.

Fast as I could, I leaped back up to my feet and turned toward where the gun had fallen. But the bald guy was already there. He grabbed the gun again and raised it, his hand trembling. This time it was pointing at me.

"Who are you?" the bald guy cried.

"He's that kid Dominic almost attacked this afternoon," Billy said, eyeing me as he got back to his feet. "I should have let him."

"Yeah, that was a bad call," I replied.

"What is he doing here?" the bald guy—Sammy, Billy had called him—asked. "How did he get here?"

"I followed Billy from his day job," I explained. "He led me straight here. Did you know your partner likes to pollute the drinking water in his spare time?"

Sam backed away from me, looking overwhelmed.

"Sam, you idiot, shoot him!" Billy hissed.

"No," Sam moaned.

They were completely focused on each other. While they were distracted, I pulled out my Swiss Army knife and chucked it toward Joe. By the time I looked back, Billy's fist was flying at my face.

I hit the ground, and his blow went over my head. As soon as I touched the rug, I swung my legs out in an arc, chopping Billy behind the knees.

He fell backward, but he'd seen it coming. He let gravity work for him, collapsing on top of me so that I took all his weight on my chest. The air left my lungs, and for a second I struggled to keep from blacking out.

Billy slammed his fist into my jaw. He pulled back to hit me again.

I rolled left, and his hand hit the rug. I kept rolling, over onto my stomach and then pushing up to a standing position.

Sam was pointing the gun right at me.

"Whoa!" I ducked again, going into a fighting crouch. "Joe, a little help?"

"One second," my brother yelled. From the corner of my eye, I could see him sawing away at Kathy's ropes with my pocketknife, holding it awkwardly with his own tied hands. I had to hand it to the guy, he was cool under pressure. Our main mission was to make sure Kathy was safe, and that's what Joe was doing. He wanted to free her so she could get away, no matter what happened to us.

Billy grabbed me from behind, wrapping his wiry arms around me and squeezing.

The guy was skinny, but he was strong. I struggled to break his hold, but I couldn't. He had my arms pinned to my sides. I was helpless.

"Get the rope," he grunted to Sam.

Sam kept the gun trained on me as he went for the unused rope on the couch. Kathy was free now, using the knife to cut Joe's bonds. But Joe turned away from her and kicked Sam's hand, getting him in the wrist. The rope slithered off the couch and onto the floor.

Sam grimaced in pain, shaking his hand. He raised the gun, aiming at Joe.

"No!" I yelled. I threw myself backward, knocking Billy off balance. The dude might be strong, but I was bigger. My weight was too much for him, and he fell. His grip on me loosened. I yanked myself away, grabbed the vase from the coffee table, and smashed it into Sam's head.

He went down, the gun went flying out of his hand, and my brother was safe.

I felt a rush of relief.

Then I heard Billy chuckle. I turned to face him.

Just as he shot me with Sam's gun.

19.

Winning Streak

"Joe!" Kathy yelled. She grabbed my hands and stabbed the knife between them with all her strength. The ropes snapped apart and I was free.

I leapt off the couch and tackled Frank just as the bullet whizzed over our heads. We hit the ground and rolled apart. No sense in giving Billy an easy target to shoot at.

Kathy ran for the phone while I jumped up and ran straight at Billy. He raised the gun to fire again, but I kept on going. I ducked my head and rammed it into his stomach. He doubled over and I grabbed on to the gun, forcing his hand back until he either had to release the gun or let his wrist snap.

He let go of the gun. I staggered back with it in my hand.

The instant I was clear, Frank hit him with a roundhouse punch. Billy's head snapped around, and he went down. Frank dove on top of him, holding him down.

I trained the gun on Billy, just in case.

"I called Security," Kathy told us. "They're on their way."

"Why don't you tie Sam's hands, just to be on the safe side," I said. The accountant was just coming to, but there was no sense in taking chances.

Kathy grabbed the rope off the floor and tied Sam up good and tight.

The door slammed open a minute later, and Gigantor stuck his head in. He spotted the gun in my hand and pulled his own weapon. He aimed at me.

"No!" Kathy said. "He's the good guy. Those are the bad guys." She pointed to Sam and Billy.

"But you can have the gun, anyway," I said, clicking on the safety and handing it to the huge security guard. "It's not mine."

Dominic Asher pushed through the door behind Gigantor. "What's going on in here?" he demanded. His gaze fell on his accountant. "Sam?" He looked at me, then at Frank. "Billy?" he added, spotting his friend underneath Frank.

"Mr. Asher, I think you should take a look at

this," I said. I pulled the printouts from my pocket. "This is from a file Sam left open on your computer. They're daily slot machine reports, and they don't match the quarterly report he showed you."

"What?" Asher frowned down at the pages. "Sam, what is he talking about?"

"Let me give you some advice. Forget about Sam and ask a real accountant to explain it to you," Kathy cut in. "And maybe take a few accounting classes yourself to make sure nobody else manages to fool you this way."

"Huh?" The Boss looked confused.

"Sam has been falsifying your books," I explained. "He and Billy rigged the slot machines so they don't pay out the amount they're supposed to by law. Then they took the extra money for themselves."

"And Sam changed my financial statements so I wouldn't notice?" Asher guessed. "Did you, Sam?"

"I couldn't have done it if you ever paid the slightest attention to numbers," Sam muttered.

The Boss's face began to flush with anger. "How dare you?" he said. "Do you have any idea how many complaints I've been getting about the slot machines? How much business I've been losing because people think my casino is crooked? I've been going around telling everybody that it was all fine. You've made me look like a liar!"

"It wasn't my idea," Sam whined. "Billy is the one who recruited me to do it."

Asher glanced at Billy. "I can't believe that," he said. "That's not true."

"It is true," I put in. "Kathy and I heard him talking to Sam about it."

"How do you know Billy, anyway?" Frank asked.

"He was my cell mate in prison," Asher replied. "I know how that sounds. But I refuse to believe Billy is involved in something like this. You have to understand—when we were in the joint, we agreed that we were both going to clean up our acts when we got out. Get jobs, keep our noses clean. I knew I had a problem with anger. Billy had gotten himself into a bad situation with organized crime. We both knew we had to change. And we promised to help each other do it."

"That's right, Dom," Billy piped up. "You're like a brother to me. You know I would never do anything to jeopardize your business."

Frank shot me a look. "Brothers don't steal from each other," he said.

"Billy didn't steal from me," Asher said. "He

would never mess with the slot machines. He knows how important the casino is to me. It's my chance to prove to my father that I can be successful."

"You know I support you in that, Dom," Billy agreed, all smiles.

"I do." Asher turned to us. "My dad is not easy to impress. He's incredibly overbearing. Billy knows that firsthand—he works for the guy."

"Wait a minute," Frank said. "Your father . . . is he Sollie Gold? Of MetaChem?"

Asher nodded. "Dad lent me the money to buy the Olde Tyme. And he gave Billy the contract to handle waste disposal for MetaChem. You might think that means he's supportive. But it doesn't. It just means he wants to keep me under his control. He's been threatening to take over the casino if it keeps losing money."

"Sollie is a pretty imposing guy," Frank agreed. "But you and he have more in common than you think. For one thing, Billy is messing with both of your businesses."

"Don't listen to these kids, Dom," Billy said. "They don't have a shred of proof that I've done anything to your slot machines."

"Unfortunately, that's true," Frank said. "Luckily, I've got terrific photos of you dumping Meta-Chem's biohazards into the water supply."

20.
Jackpot

"It's a twisted tale of high-stakes corruption, stretching from the glamour of a casino resort to the quiet shores of a forest stream," Joe read aloud. "From the cutting edge of scientific research to the old-time theme of a Mississippi riverboat." He paused and grinned at me over the top of the newspaper.

"She's good," I said. "The girl can write."

Kathy's article had appeared in this morning's *Press of Atlantic City.* She must have been up all night writing it, but who could blame her? Two ex-cons who go on to be involved with illegal toxic dumping and rigged slot machines at a glitzy resort—it was a good story. Throw in a little murder, a little kidnapping, and a daring rescue, and you had front-page news. Too bad she couldn't mention her saviors by name.

"I think I'll read the rest later," Joe said. "It's too nice out to waste my time on the news."

I followed his gaze to a couple of girls on the other side of the Olde Tyme's pool. They were watching us and giggling. Joe grinned and waved.

"So you'd rather flirt with strangers than read Kathy's story?" I teased him.

Joe shrugged. "I know how the story ends."

A shadow fell over my lounge chair. I looked up to see Dominic Asher.

"Hi, boys," he said. "I'm glad to see you took me up on the offer to stay at the Olde Tyme for another day."

"Are you kidding?" Joe said. "We were so busy working that we didn't get to do any of the cool things here. I mean, this is the first time we're even getting to see the pool."

"It is really outrageous," I agreed. "I love that it has a river attached, with a current and everything." The fake "river" snaked all around the patio area and fed into the pool at the end.

"And the rafts are a stroke of genius," Joe added.

The Boss laughed. "Thank you. And I'm happy to say that the phones have been ringing off the hook all morning with new reservations. It seems that Kathy's article has made a lot of people aware of the Olde Tyme Resort and Casino. Who would have thought that a story about crooked gambling would make people want to come stay here?"

"Any publicity is good publicity," Joe said.

"Besides, you weren't the one messing with the slot machines," I pointed out. "The Olde Tyme shouldn't have to suffer just because Sam messed up. This place is really cool. You've done a great job with it."

"That's what I want to hear," Asher replied. "It's not just about gambling. I want the whole family to be able to have fun here."

"Any word on Doreen McKenzie?" Joe asked.

"Yes, the police chief called me twenty minutes ago to say they had arrested her," Asher said. "Needless to say, she's also been fired by the Gaming Commissioner."

"It sounds like everything is taken care of," I said.

Asher took a deep breath and gazed around the pool area, grinning. "Yep. I feel like a new man," he said. "I spent all the time since I got out of prison telling myself I wanted to change, be a better person. Now I realize that I have. And it's all thanks to you two."

"So you're doing okay without Billy?" I asked. "We know he was your go-to guy for moral support."

"At least I thought he was." Dominic sighed. "I really thought he had changed since prison, but I guess some people are always going to be bad. Still, I've got something better now. I've got my dad's respect. He called me as soon as he heard about Billy, just to say he's proud of me. I think he was surprised that I actually wasn't involved in the slot machine scam. He's always thought of me as a rotten apple, ever since I got sent to jail."

"He didn't believe you could change?" Joe guessed.

"Nope. I think he was afraid that if he trusted me, I would only disappoint him again."

"That's not entirely true," I pointed out. "He did give you the money to buy the Olde Tyme. He was willing to back your business, so he must have trusted you a little."

"Or at least he wanted to trust you," Joe agreed.

Dominic smiled. "I never thought about it that way. I guess he did want to trust me. And now he knows that he can."

"I bet he's relieved that the illegal dumping charge isn't going to go against MetaChem too," I said.

"That's for sure." Dominic winked. "I should go. My dad is actually meeting me here for lunch. You boys have fun."

I pulled out my cell phone.

"Are you calling that MetaChem girl?" Joe asked. "What was her name?"

"Lucy. Lou." I felt embarrassed just thinking about her. "No, I was going to call Edna Williams."

"Really? You'd rather date an old lady than a hot girl?" Joe teased me.

I smacked his arm. "I just want to tell Edna that she's safe now. She can join the rest of the people from the retirement home on their weekly visit again."

"I'm sure she read about it in the paper," Joe said. "I think you need to call Lou. Didn't you tell me you promised her a dinner date?"

"Yeah," I muttered. Lou was definitely cute. But what would we even talk about at dinner? The whole idea made me nervous.

"Tell you what," Joe said. "I'll spend some time flirting with the girls here today until I find one I like enough to ask out."

"You mean until you find one who takes pity on you and actually says yes," I corrected him.

"Right," Joe said. "And then we can double date. We can have dinner at the restaurant here at the Olde Tyme."

"Okay." I frowned at the cell phone. "I'll call her in an hour. If you've managed to find a date. I don't think I can handle a one-on-one dinner with Lou."

"An hour? No problem," Joe said. Then he nodded toward the hotel doors. "Check it out."

I looked and saw Sollie Gold standing there, peering out over the crowded pool area. I had never seen the big guy look so happy before.

Dominic walked over and greeted his dad with a big hug.

"That's nice to see," I commented.

"Sure is," Joe replied. "Family has to stick together."

"You said it." I grinned at my brother. "Now let's hit that rooftop roller coaster!"

Turn the page for a sneak peak at the all-new

THE UNDERCOVER BROTHERS®

HARDY BOYS

GIRL DETECTIVE®

NANCY DREW

Super Mystery

TERROR ON TOUR

FRANK

A NEW MISSION

"Pop it in, already!" Joe said.

I glanced at him. He was jumping around like an overcaffeinated monkey. Then again, that could pretty well describe my brother most of the time. He isn't what you'd call patient.

"I'm working on it," I told him.

I couldn't resist slowing my movements a little just to bug him. First I slid the CD slooowly out from between the pages of the ad booklet. I took my time as I made a leisurely stroll across my bedroom toward the game console on my desk. My hand moved like molasses as I reached toward the power button. . . .

"*Frank!*" Joe exclaimed.

I grinned. Joe is way too easy to mess with sometimes.

But I didn't make him suffer any longer. I was just as eager as he was to see what our next mission would be. I slid the CD into the machine and hit Play.

"Greetings, ATAC agents," said the familiar voice of Q., our boss at ATAC. *"Your next mission begins in six days, and involves out-of-state travel. Please press Continue if you would like to accept the mission. Your briefing will follow."*

"No brainer." Joe lunged for the console and pressed the button.

I opened my mouth to remind him that we're supposed to be a team, and that it would be nice if he consulted me before pressing Continue. Or before climbing through a window in an abandoned house, for that matter.

But then I shut it again. Joe will never change. Besides, the message was starting.

A silvery flash filled the screen, and the ear-shattering scream of an electric guitar poured out of the speakers. I cast a nervous glance at the bedroom door, hoping Mom and Aunt Trudy were still safely downstairs.

When I looked at the screen again, it was filled with smoke. A dark figure strode out from the middle of it, carrying a microphone. He had shaggy dark hair and was wearing leather pants and a mask.

"Hello ATAC agents!" the mystery man on the screen shrieked into the microphone. *"Are you ready to rock? Because you're going to Rockapazooma!"*

"Whoa!" Joe exclaimed as the masked guy paused to

play a sizzling lick on his guitar. "Did you hear that? Rockapazooma!"

"Isn't that some big concert out in the Midwest?" I said. "I saw something about it on TV the other day."

Joe looked shocked. "It's not just *some* concert, dude," he said. "It's *the* concert!"

I shrugged. I like music as much as the next guy, but I'm not obsessed with it like Joe. He wears his DJ Razz T-shirt all the time. Aunt Trudy has forbidden him from wearing his Lethal Injection shirt, though. For some reason she thinks the picture of one band member holding up another band member's severed head is disgusting.

Onscreen, the guitar-playing guy was fading out. He was replaced by the image of crowds of people partying at an outdoor concert.

Q.'s voice continued the message in voice-over. *"Rockapazooma is more than just the biggest concert of the year. It's a way for musicians and sponsors to raise awareness of the environmental problems facing the world today: deforestation, endangered species, global warming, and other issues. All proceeds of the show will go to groups working to fight these problems. So not only will fans get to enjoy an entire day of great live music, but they'll be helping to save the world, too. Sounds like a win-win, right?"*

"Totally," Joe interjected with a grin. "Especially for us!"

"However," the voice continued, *"ATAC and its affiliated agencies have intercepted buzz indicating that someone may intend to disrupt the concert. Unfortunately we can't tell you much more than that. The stakes are high, and if the wrong people were to intercept this message, it could endanger the mission—and your lives."*

"Helpful," I commented.

Joe was grinning. "I can't believe we're really going to Rockapazooma!"

Way to stay on task, I thought. But I didn't say anything, because the voice-over was continuing.

"Your identities for this mission are Jack and Jimmy Leyland, ordinary music fans. You will have to stay on the lookout for anything suspicious. We may try to mobilize another set of agents to work on this case as well, but you should proceed as if you are the only agents present. We are working closely with the local police department and FBI office on this case, so if you run into any serious trouble, please consider them your allies. A crowd-control tool is included in the CD case in case you run into any trouble. As usual this mission is top secret. Good luck, and rock on, ATACers. This CD will be reformatted in five seconds. Five, four, three, two, one . . ."

I steeled myself for more screaming guitars when the disk switched to music. Instead, a female voice poured out of the speakers. The song was catchy, but I didn't recognize it.

"Who's this?" I asked.

Joe stared at me. "Man, you're even more out of touch than I thought. It's only the Royal We, the hottest new band in the known world."

"The Royal We?" It rang a bell. "Wait, isn't that the band with the young female singer—"

"Who's amazingly hot?" Joe finished for me. "Yeah, her name's Kijani."

"I was going to say, the young female singer who sought asylum here from her home country in Africa." I searched my mind for the details. I'd read a story on the singer a few weeks ago in a news magazine. "She's part of a royal family, I think. That's how they came up with the idea for the name of the band."

"Whatever." Joe shrugged.

"Joe, we're not going to Rockapazooma to look at girls," I reminded him.

Joe grinned. "The guy on the CD said to watch out for anything suspicious," he said. "I'll be keeping my eye out for suspiciously hot girls."

I suddenly remembered something. "Hey, didn't the CD say something was included with it?" I grabbed for the jewel case, which I'd dropped on the desk near the game console.

Joe looked over my shoulder as I examined it. "What is it?" he asked. "Must be pretty small."

"Here we go." I spotted two cylindrical silvery objects tucked into the casing. Each was about the size and shape of a pack of breath mints. Joe grabbed one and I picked up the other.

I turned it over in my hands. The only thing breaking the smooth silver surface was a tiny button at one end. "I wonder how they—"

"*YOW!*" Joe yelled, jumping about three feet in the air. He dropped his tool and shook his right hand violently, hopping up and down and grimacing. "That thing has a serious *bite* to it! Take my advice, Frank—don't touch the end and press the button at the same time."

That's my brother—the human guinea pig. "So they're like miniature cattle prods." I figured that could definitely come in handy in a crowd full of rowdy concert-goers.

"Boys?" Aunt Trudy's voice floated through the door. "Is everything okay in there? What's with all the yelling?"

"We're fine, Aunt Trudy," I called back. "Sorry about the noise."

As her footsteps faded away, I looked at Joe. "That reminds me. How're we going to explain this one?"

Keeping our ATAC work a secret from Mom and Aunt Trudy is always a challenge. Dad helps us cover when he can. But mostly Joe and I just need to be really good at coming up with stories to explain our comings and goings.

"Easy," Joe said. "We tell the truth—sort of."

I blinked. "Huh?"

Joe grinned. "We say we're going to Rockapazooma,"

he said. "Lethal Injection and DJ Razz are both playing the show. Everybody knows I'm into them. So we say I called in to a radio contest or something, and won an all-expenses-paid trip for two to the show."

I had to admit it was a great plan. "Keep it simple," I said, echoing one of Dad's favorite sayings. "Yeah, that could work." Then I realized what he'd said and grimaced. "Lethal Injection, huh?"

"Yeah! I can't wait to see them live," Joe exclaimed. "It's going to be awesome! I wonder what the death stunt will be? Oh! And I hope they play 'White Hot Death'—that song rocks."

I couldn't help grinning at his enthusiasm, even if I didn't share it. "Yeah," I said. "Remind me to pack my earplugs, okay?"

"Whoa!" Joe climbed out of the taxi. "Check it out. This place is packed already."

I finished paying the driver. Then I straightened up and looked around.

Joe was right. The concert venue was a seething mass of humanity. Now that we were there, there was no question about why we might need those crowd-control devices if we were to do any investigating. We weren't even inside and we could barely move.

We were standing near the parking area, which was bumper to grill with vehicles. A tall chain-link fence blocked off the enormous field where the concert would take place. Through it I could see a huge stage surrounded by an equally huge spiderweb of lights and rigging. Sixty-foot-tall speaker towers stood on either side of the stage. Giant video screens atop more speakers dotted the football-field-size area in front of it.

I could also see people. Lots of people.

"And here I thought we were arriving nice and early," I said. "The music doesn't even start for more than an hour!"

"Well, we're here now." Joe headed toward the nearest entry point. "Let's get inside."

We waited in line for our turn. A bored-looking security guard glanced at our passes, which we'd picked up from the pilot of the private plane that had flown us in from Bayport that morning.

"Welcome to Rockapazooma." The guard stifled a yawn. He was wearing a neon green T-shirt with the concert's logo—a smiling planet Earth playing an electric guitar. It was kind of dorky, but it got the point across. "Are you carrying any liquids, weapons, or electronic devices?"

"No way," Joe answered for both of us. We took out our cell phones and pocket change and put them in the guy's little tray.

"Step through the metal detector and enjoy the show."

I thought about the mini-electric-prod in my jeans pocket. What if the metal detector picked it up and we got kicked out?

But I should have known ATAC would be on top of things. We both made it through the metal detector without a buzz.

"Guess those little shocker doodads don't have much metal in them," Joe commented as we stepped away.

"Yeah." I stuck my cell back in my pocket and glanced around. From inside the gates the place looked even more crowded. "I guess we should still follow our original plan—walk around and try to get a feel for the place before it gets any busier."

"Are you sure?" Joe teased. "You mean, you don't have a backup plan?"

I didn't bother to answer. I was still feeling kind of uneasy about the whole situation. It was weird not knowing what this mission was about. There had been times when ATAC had been more vague with us than I would have liked, but this took the cake.

Still, that didn't mean we couldn't attack it logically. Right?

"Let's make a circuit of the whole place," I suggested. "We can scope out the best places to see the crowd."

"The crowd?" Joe glanced toward the stage. A bunch

of roadies were up there moving equipment around. "What about the bands?"

I started walking. "We're not here to watch the bands."

"We're supposed to keep an eye on *everything*," Joe pointed out. "That means the bands too."

"Whatever." I stopped and shaded my eyes against the sun. "Let's head for that speaker tower out in the middle first, and then—"

"Hey!" Joe grabbed my arm. "Check out the babe."

A young woman of about nineteen was doing some kind of solo interpretive dance nearby. Her eyes were closed, and her arms were waving over her head. She was dressed in nothing but a grass skirt and a skimpy bikini top that left very little to the imagination.

"We're not here for *that*, either," I told Joe. "Come on."

Joe shot one last glance at the teen. Then he jogged to catch up with me.

"You're not going to let me have any fun at all on this trip, are you?"

He was giving me the Look. I hate the Look. It makes me feel like I'm a hundred and one years older than Joe, instead of just one. It almost made me ashamed that I really *had* packed earplugs for this trip. They were in my jeans pocket right now, right next to the mini-cattle-prod. Good thing Joe didn't know that. Otherwise I'd probably be facing the Look times ten.

But I couldn't let it get to me. We had business to take care of. "Grow up, Joe," I told him. "We're here on a case, remember?"

"Yeah, I know," he said. "But that doesn't mean we can't have fun, too."

We were still moving through the crowd as we talked. At that moment we were off to the right side of the stage. Just ahead I noticed several security guards wearing those neon green planet shirts. They were standing in front of another chain-link fence. Behind it were a bunch of big gleaming charter-type buses and double-wide trailers.

Joe spotted them too. "That looks like the backstage area," he said. "Let's sneak in and take a look."

"Sneak in?" I glanced at the guards. Each of them alone easily weighed more than Joe and I did together. "I don't think so."

"Why not?" Joe said. "You're the one who's always saying we should be thorough, and—whoa! Check *her* out!"

Glancing where he was staring, I saw three girls about our own age. Unlike Ms. Bikini Dancer, they were all fully clothed in shorts and T-shirts. The slim girl with reddish-blond hair and the athletic-looking brunette were both cute. But their friend really stood out in the crowd. She was blond and curvy, with the kind of face that made you want to walk right up to her and say hi.

I realized I was staring. I also realized that Joe was already hurrying toward the girls.

Uh-oh. I took off after him.

"Hi," he was saying to the blond when I caught up. "I'm Joe. What's your—"

"Excuse us," I interrupted.

I grabbed his arm. He struggled a little, but I dragged him away.

The blond girl giggled and waved. Her dark-haired friend rolled her eyes.

"Dorks," she muttered.

The third girl, the one with the reddish hair, just watched us go. She looked amused.

"What's the big idea?" Joe finally broke free of my grip. He looked around for the girls, but they'd already been swallowed up in the crowd. "Those three looked suspicious. I was just going to question them a little."

"Yeah, right." I let out a snort. "Get your hormones under control, Mr. Slick. We've got work to do."

Joe snapped to attention and saluted. "Sir, yes sir!"

Just then there was a commotion up ahead. A camera crew was emerging from the backstage area. They were surrounding a gorgeous young woman holding a microphone. I recognized her as Annie Wu, a VJ from the music television station. Fans were pushing forward, trying to catch a better look at the VJ. As soon as the crew was through, the guards returned to their positions in front of the backstage gate.

"We really need to get in there," Joe said. "Let's see if we can find a weak spot in the fence."

At least he was back on track with the mission. "Okay," I said. "Can't hurt to check it out."

I still wasn't sure trying to sneak in was the best use of our time right then. But at least it would distract Joe from girls for a few minutes.

Less than ten minutes later we were in. It wasn't even a challenge to our ATAC skills—we just walked along the fence until we came to a spot where two sections of the fence came together. Or rather, where they *didn't* come together. They were hooked to each other with a chain, but there was a space between them just big enough for us to squeeze through. There was a green-shirted guard nearby, but he was talking on a cell phone with his back to us, so we got through easily.

Once we were inside, nobody paid any attention to us. There were tons of people running around, looking busy and important. We started walking, taking in the whole scene.

"Look," I said. "That must be the official press area."

There were a bunch of big portable lights set up around a small stage containing a couple of director's chairs with the Rockapazooma logo on them. A neon green screen stood behind the stage.

Joe glanced that way and nodded. "Guess nobody's getting interviewed right now," he said. "Come on, let's check out the band trailers."

We wandered deeper into the backstage area. Trailers, buses, and semis loomed all around us. There were fewer people walking around in this section, although there were big, muscular guys guarding some of the trailers and buses.

After turning a corner we passed a large but nondescript trailer. Just ahead I noticed a cotton-candy pink tour bus painted with airy white swirls.

"Wonder which band came in that thing?" I said.

"Bet it wasn't DJ Razz." Joe grinned. "If he was seen in a bus like that, his fans would disown him."

I laughed. "Yeah, but what better way to travel incognito?" I said. "Nobody would ever guess Razz was inside that Barbie-doll-looking thing."

"True." Joe glanced over at the generic-looking trailer we were passing at the moment. "But I still bet he'd rather—"

Joe was cut off by a sudden, bloodcurdling scream.

CHANCE ENCOUNTERS

Ned had to be at the concert early. Bess, George, and I weren't complaining about that. We were so psyched to be at Rockapazooma that we were all about to burst.

"I need to go sign in at the press tent," Ned told us after we cleared the metal detector at the entrance gate. "Want to come along? I can try to get you guys backstage with me."

"Awesome!" George's eyes sparkled. "Maybe we'll see Nick Needles or Mike Manslaughter walking around!"

"Mike Manslaughter?" Bess wrinkled her nose. "Let me guess—another member of Lethal Injection?"

"Duh. He's only the lead singer." George tugged on Ned's arm. "Come on, let's go!"

We wound our way through the crowd. I couldn't believe it was already so packed. The show wouldn't start for almost ninety minutes, but it looked as if at least half of the expected 200,000 people were already there. Some people had set up folding chairs in front of the stage, while others were lying out in the sun on picnic blankets or tossing Frisbees or playing Hacky Sack. There were long lines at the refreshment stands and the souvenir booths, and even longer ones at the restrooms.

"Wow," I said. "This is wild! I can't believe we're really here."

Ned reached over and squeezed my hand. "Having fun so far?"

"Definitely." I smiled and squeezed back. "I just can't believe how crowded it is. Good thing we brought cell phones in case we get separated. Because there's no way you could ever find someone in this . . ."

My voice trailed off as I spotted the backstage gate, which was just a few yards ahead now. Was I seeing things?

"What's wrong?" Ned asked.

Bess blinked. "Is that Deirdre?" she exclaimed.

There was no mistaking it. A line of security guards dressed in neon green shirts with the concert logo on them were standing in front of the gate. Deirdre was glaring up at one of them, a man approximately the same size and shape as a refrigerator. He stared at her impassively, his meaty arms crossed over his chest. I guessed that his green T-shirt had to be a size XXXL.

"Oh, man," George muttered, staring at Deirdre in disbelief. "We've been here twenty minutes, and look who we run into. What are the odds?"

I shook my head. "I don't know. But it looks like maybe that backstage pass of hers isn't working too well."

We hurried forward. Deirdre was waving her hands around and whining at the huge guard. Now that we were closer, I could see that the name tag pinned to the guard's shirt identified him as TYREESE—SECURITY.

". . . and if you had more than two brain cells to rub together, you'd realize that I'm obviously telling the truth," Deirdre was complaining as we got close enough to overhear. "I was told quite clearly that this ticket gives me free admission to the *entire* concert grounds. And that obviously means I should be able to go backstage without some oversized rent-a-guard stopping me, and . . ."

As we all listened in, George's expression changed from annoyance to delight. Finally she stepped forward.

"Well, hello, DeeDee," she said. "Having some problems, are we?"

Deirdre spun around, looking startled. "Oh, it's you," she spat. "Mind your own business. I'm just trying to explain to this doofus that I need to get backstage." She spun around to glare at the guard again. "Just wait until my friends Kijani and Nicky Needles hear about this. Oh, and Toni Lovely, too. They're all close friends of mine, you know. Did you hear me? Once my good friend Kijani hears about this, you'll never work security in this town again!"

The guard didn't look impressed by her threat. "Nobody gets backstage without the proper authorization," he rumbled in a deep voice. "Not without going through me first."

Ned shot me an amused glance. "Maybe this isn't the best time to try to get you guys backstage after all," he murmured.

George heard the guard too. She looked disappointed, but she nodded. "We'll have to meet up with you later."

"Definitely." Ned patted the cell phone clipped to his belt. "See you."

He stepped past Deirdre, who was still ranting at the top of her lungs. Approaching one of the other guards, Ned held up his press pass. The guard peered at it, then waved him through.

"See you, Ned!" George sang out loudly, waving at him. "Have fun backstage!"

Deirdre heard and shot her a dirty look. George smiled pleasantly in return. "You too, Deirdre," she said sweetly. "*If* you ever get back there, that is."

Bess grabbed her by the arm and dragged her away.

"Come on," she chided with a smile. "Stop teasing Deirdre. It's not nice."

"Says who?" George grinned.

Just then I noticed a guy around our age charging toward us. He was cute, with wavy blond hair and blue eyes. "Who's that?" I asked my friends. "Someone you know?"

Bess and George both shook their heads. "Looks like he wants to know us, though," George commented. "*One* of us, anyway."

As he got closer, it became obvious that the blond guy was staring at Bess. That was nothing new. With her blond hair, great figure, and dimples, Bess turns heads wherever she goes. Guys are always coming up to her on the street, in restaurants, at the mall, in the post office—pretty much anywhere. Luckily Bess never lets all the attention go to her head. In fact, she kind of hates it.

The guy skidded to a stop in front of us. "Hi," he said breathlessly, his eyes locked on to Bess. "I'm Joe. What's your—"

"Excuse us."

Another guy had suddenly appeared. He was a little taller and leaner than the blond guy, but just as good-looking, with dark hair and an intense expression on his angular face. Without another word, he grabbed the first guy's arm and yanked him away.

Bess giggled and waved as the two guys moved away.

"Dorks," George muttered, rolling her eyes.

I just watched in amusement as the blond guy struggled against his friend's grip. "Too bad, Bess," I commented as the two guys were lost behind a group of teenagers batting around a beach ball. "Those guys were pretty cute."

Just then Deirdre's voice floated toward us from back by the gate. "Fine!" she shrieked. "You win, okay? But this isn't the last you've seen of me! As soon as I get in touch with Kijani and Nick, I'll be back!"

I glanced over that way just in time to see Deirdre storm off, her face frozen in a furious scowl. She pushed between a couple of the beach-ball-tossing teens.

"Yo!" one of them said in surprise. "Watch it!"

"Watch it yourself," Deirdre snarled, not slowing her pace as she stalked off into the crowd.

"Come on." George was already heading off after her. "If her head's about to explode, I want to be there to see it."

I had to admit I was at least mildly curious about what Deirdre would do next. As I've already mentioned, she isn't the type to give up easily on something she wants.

"Okay, why not," I said. "We still have a while until the concert starts."

"Oh, Nancy." Bess sounded amused. "You'll do anything to pretend you have a mystery to solve."

I shrugged and grinned. "You're right," I told Bess with a smile. "It's the mystery of how Deirdre Shannon is going to enjoy herself at this concert if she can't get backstage to rub elbows with the stars."

George gestured to us impatiently. "Hurry up—we're losing her!"

Even in the ever-growing crowd it wasn't too difficult to keep track of Deirdre. All we had to do was follow the chorus of *Hey*s and *Watch it*s and *Ow*s she left in her wake as she rudely pushed past people. It also helped that she was wearing a hot pink shirt with yellow trim. Deirdre likes to stand out.

We stayed back a few yards, trying not to let her see us while keeping her in sight. As we walked, we also had a chance to look around and to see more of the concert area.

Deirdre's path was leading us deeper into the crowd in front of the stage, which had grown thicker as the concert's start time drew closer. People were sitting, standing, dancing, or wandering across the field. Here and there we could see the bright green of a security guard's T-shirt among them. Up on the stage, workers were setting up microphones and busily moving equipment back and forth. The atmosphere, which had been relaxed when we arrived, was sizzling with anticipation.

"Hey, look!" Bess said, pointing as one of the video screens hanging over the huge stage flickered to life. It showed the Rockapazooma logo for a moment or two, then started flashing images of trees, wildlife, oceans, and other scenes of nature.

"Almost time!" George had to raise her voice to be heard over the buzz of conversation, laughter, and random outbursts of singing all around us.

I glanced ahead, catching a glimpse of Deirdre's pink shirt. She had just passed the nearest large speaker tower, which was located in the middle of the front section of the audience area about fifty yards from the stage. Judging by the direction she was going, I guessed she was heading for the line of refreshment stands off to the left side of the stage area.

"Maybe we should start looking for a spot to watch from," Bess suggested. "It looks like we're losing Deirdre anyway."

Turning to glance once more toward the speaker tower, I saw that she was right. Deirdre had disappeared behind a cluster of middle-aged men who were tossing around a football.

"Okay," I said. "Where do you want to go?"

Bess opened her mouth, but her answer was drowned out as the speakers suddenly crackled to life. There was a burst of music, then a voice: "Testing, testing—earth, air, sea . . ."

The crowd reacted immediately, letting out an excited roar. All around us, people surged forward, everyone trying to get closer to the stage.

Bess grabbed my hand. "Come on!" she yelled. "Let's go this way!"

I nodded and started to follow. But something made me glance over toward that speaker tower again—the last place I'd seen Deirdre. At that moment several of the middle-aged men tackled one of their friends, and I could see past them to the base of the metal tower.

There was a flash of hot pink. Deirdre?

"Come on, Nancy!" George shouted in my ear, giving me a shove.

"Wait!" I said, though I doubted anyone could hear me—the speakers had just emitted another ear-shattering burst of music.

But I yanked free of Bess's hand, straining to see through the crowd. There it was again—the flash of pink.

I gasped. It *was* Deirdre . . . and she was shrieking and struggling as an enormous man in a green security T-shirt roughly dragged her off.